Endure

By

Nate Johnson

Purple Herb Publishing

AuthorNateJo@gmail.com

https://www.facebook.com/AuthorNateJo/

Dedicated to
Miss Riley Neva
Wilkinson

Other books by Nate Johnson

Endure

Chapter One

<u>Chase</u>

I'll be honest. I'm not exactly a people-type person. That was why I was up in the High Sierra mountains. But no way did I want the world to end. Even I'm not that much of a loner.

I was squatting next to the campfire pouring my one vice, coffee, when my cell phone buzzed with my uncle's ringtone, shocking me. I was surprised it still had power, let alone coverage. But Tahoe was only a dozen miles away, so I guess I was close enough.

Sighing, I answered, "Uncle Frank, is everything okay?" I honestly couldn't think of why he'd be calling otherwise, he knew I just wanted to be left alone.

"Blue Jester," he said with a resigned tone.

Holy crap, I thought. This wasn't going to be good.

He cleared his throat then said, "Are you still up in the mountains? High up?"

"Yes."

"Good, stay there."

I scoffed. "I'm two hours from the nearest road. What is going on."

He sighed heavily. "The asteroid ..."

"What asteroid?" I asked. I'd been offline for a week.

"We're going to be hit by an asteroid. A big one. Soon. I think it's going to hit in the Pacific."

My gut tightened. Uncle Frank was an astrophysicist, who taught at the University of Washington up in Seattle. If he said it was going to hit. We were going to get clobbered. "How bad?" I asked as I held my breath waiting for the answer.

"Bad," he said with resignation. "A civilization-ending type. Think EMP, Floods, Earthquakes. Every disaster imaginable. I've already called Ryan and Haley. I've told them both to get to Papa's farm in Idaho."

"How?" I barked. "Haley's on the other side of the country. Ryan's a mile from a beach that's going to get drowned by the biggest tsunami in the history of tsunamis.

"I know," he said, and I could hear the fear and resignation in his voice. "I'm hear at JPL ..."

"What? In California? That's close to the beach. What are you doing down there?"

"Listen, Chase, I don't have time to explain. You know what this means. Get to

Idaho. They're going to need you. I've got to call Cassie, she's visiting the Thompsons in Oklahoma."

My stomach clenched up. He was serious. This was end of the world stuff. "But ..." I started only I couldn't think of what to say.

"You're a good man," he said with a tone that tore at my heart. "Your mom and dad would have been proud of you. I know I am." I knew he meant it. But I also knew he wouldn't be saying it if he ever expected to see me again.

"Get out of there," I told him as an anger began to build inside of me. First off, he was too valuable to be putting himself at risk. Next. How dare the world do this to us? My family. No, it wasn't right.

"I've got to go," he said. "I love you. Get to Idaho." There was a sudden click and then a soul-eating silence on the other end.

"Uncle Frank?" I gasped. But nothing, he was gone.

I froze, looking down at the fire, trying to think, trying to process what I had just been told. An asteroid? What would it mean? According to my uncle, the end of the world. Hey, I was enough of a loner that I'd read all the doomsday books. Everything from The Stand to the Earth Abides. I knew what happened.

7

Technology died, which means the people died. Those that weren't killed outright by the disaster itself. The world couldn't support eight billion people without our current level of technology. Everything from transportation to fertilizer. From medicine to electricity. Things were going to get real bad, real fast.

And when things got bad, people took it out on each other. It would become a dog-eat-dog world rather quickly.

Shaking my head, I tried to wrap my mind around it. But I kept coming up against a brick wall. I was in central California, it the middle of the wilderness. The smart move would be to stay here, away from people. I had fishing gear, camping stuff, and snares. I knew the forest. I could last six months until late fall.

But then what? No way was I surviving a winter. Besides, my family needed me. My cousins Ryan and Cassie, and my sister Haley. God, my insides squeezed shut. How could she possibly make it from New York to Idaho? I'd never see her again. I'd never know what happened to her.

Without thinking it through, I tried calling her. I needed to hear her voice. The phone just rang and rang as a guilty sick feeling filled me. I was her older brother. I should have been there to protect her. But instead, I was off sulking in the high mountains of California.

"Come on, answer," I said as I stared down at my phone.

A sudden sadness filled me. How many people were going to die? How many of them were the people I cared about?

"What now?" I mumbled to myself. I was safe up here. Unless the thing was a direct hit. I'd be fine. But what about the long term? My uncle was right. I needed to get to Papa's farm. If our family was ever to be together it would be there.

Tossing my coffee onto the fire I kicked it dead then poured the pot of coffee on it and started tearing my tent down. By the time I had everything packed the fire was cold. Shouldering my pack I started towards I-80. There was a rest stop just east of Truckee, I'd try to catch a ride into Reno, then work my way north to Idaho. If I had to walk, if I pushed it, I could be there in three weeks, four if things got bad. Boy was I wrong.

I wasn't a hundred yards down the trail when a bright light lit the sky like a second sun west of me. Over the Pacific. I winced and looked away then felt a shiver rush down my spine. Uncle Frank had been right, and we were so screwed.

A sick sourness filled my gut as I began to truly realize what was going to happen and how bad it was going to be. Holding my breath I pulled out my phone. Deader than dead. There had been enough power left it should still be working. But nope. That meant EMP. No doubt about it.

Taking a moment I slowly turned and looked at the forest. Tall ponderosa pines. Dry grass. Snow on the slopes up above me, a couple of weeks from the last of it melting. Nothing had changed. A red cardinal hoped to a higher branch. A squirrel chirped, warning his friends that I was in his area. The wind ruffled the grass.

My brain knew that my world had changed. But there was no sign of it. Mother Nature didn't care. She was going about doing her thing. It was us humans that were screwed. We'd spent ten thousand years creating civilization. A way of life that harnessed resources and turned them to our benefit.

A society that had tamed the world and forced it to our will.

Barking a laugh, I shook my head. One little rock from space and everything was gone. I remembered a conversation between my Dad and Uncle Frank. I'd been ten and sat quietly on the back porch while they drank beers and talked about what would happen if we ever got hit by an EMP.

I had been so afraid they'd send me into the house. Or stop talking because this was grownup talk. But they'd ignored me. I think Dad wanted me to hear this stuff. It was one of those life-changing moments as I began to realize what it meant to be a man.

I learned about responsibility, looking problems in the eye, not flinching. And the importance of being prepared. Not just physically, but mentally. Spiritually. And I had failed miserably. My family was scattered all over the country. And I was up here in the mountains where I couldn't help anyone.

Three years later Mom and Dad were dead. Along with Aunt Jenny. And again, my life changed. This time a permanent anger took control of me. Burrowing deep into my soul and refusing to let go.

An anger at the world. At people. At anything and everything.

I guess that flash of light was another life-changing event. Now I had something new to be angry at. I mean, the world ending will ruin a person's life. Stone cold fact.

Taking a deep breath, I shifted my pack then started down the trail. A sudden urgency filled me. I needed to get to Idaho. I had a mission. A reason to focus. My cousins and my sister might need me. No, they would need me. We would have to rely on each other if we were going to survive this.

Of course, fifteen minutes later the ground decided to throw me off its back. I swear I was lifted a dozen feet then the ground dropped out from beneath me. EARTHQUAKE I thought as I hugged the ground.

"You're outside," I said to myself as the ground shook left then right like a terrier with a rat. A deep rumble, like an approaching train, echoed off the mountains as the ground continued to shake.

I held on, letting the earth throw its tantrum, knowing I couldn't be hurt too bad. Then the rumble shifted, became more focused. A sick fear filled me as I looked up the mountain to see a section of the hillside and snow let go.

"Crap," I yelled as I pushed up and turned, placing my back to the avalanche racing down the mountain.

"Go, go," I screamed as I tried to run while the earth continued to shake, slamming me into a tree. Holding my breath, I glanced over my shoulder to see the avalanche picking up trees and turning them into toothpicks.

Suddenly, the earth stopped shaking, allowing me to run in a straight line. My pack felt like a ton of bricks as it bounced into my back. I was tempted to drop it, but I'd never survive the end of the world without my stuff. So I ran and prayed. The first thing I'd asked for since my parents had been killed.

Shifting, I turned to the side to race uphill. If I could make that ridge, I might be okay. The Avalanche wouldn't crest it. Would it?

Really, there was only one way to find out. Forcing my legs like pistons I pushed myself up the slope as the rumble behind me increased, drawing nearing, a tumbling rumble that foreshadowed my death.

Ignoring the noise, I pushed myself, gasping for air, using my hands to pull myself up the last ten yards to flop down on the crest, sucking in air. Turning, I watched the avalanche finish coming down then start up the opposite ridge towards me before turning to the side, Searching for an easier path down the mountains.

Flopping back I stared up into the sky. An hour. One hour and I was almost dead. This new world was filled with hidden dangers. How was I ever going to make Idaho?

Chapter Two

<u>Meagan</u>

Mom had looked terrible, I thought. But then, prison will do that to a woman. Glancing in the rearview mirror I saw that my brothers, Jimmy, and Austin, were each lost in their own world. Staring out the car's windows at the passing trees.

Squeezing the steering wheel, I forced myself to focus on the road. We'd just passed through Truckee, headed down the east side of the Sierras, and would be home in an hour. "We'll be there soon, Nanny," I whispered under my breath.

We lived with our grandmother in Reno Nevada. Our dad's mother. We'd visited Mom in the Folsom Women's Correctional facility yesterday, not the most welcoming of places. Then stayed at a Holiday Inn. We were supposed to go back there this morning, but Nanny had called. She'd fallen again and needed me home.

Glancing back at the boys I let out a long sigh. That was probably the last time we'd ever visit Mom. I know she said she never meant to do it. But some things are just unforgivable. I had thought, maybe, maybe she could convince me. But no. I could hear it in her voice. She wasn't really sorry. Oh, she was sorry for getting caught. But not for killing my dad.

An anger burned my guts as I forced it back down. Calm breaths, I thought to myself. The shrinks had taught me to control my breathing and it actually worked sometimes. Or It did until everything went wrong?

There was a quick flash then the car stopped working. I don't just mean the engine. But everything. The steering felt like it had frozen solid, It took all my effort to turn the wheel just the slightest. The brakes were like stomping on a mushy toad then hard brick.

"Meagan," Jimmy called like maybe I didn't know I was headed straight for a guard rail. The brakes were useless. Luckily, I was able to crank the wheel just enough so we hit at a glancing blow. Unfortunately, it was enough for the airbag to explode, and my world burst into a thousand stars dancing around my head.

The scrunch of metal and the explosion of the airbag mixed with white powdery talcum all worked to confuse me as I tried to understand what had happened. My face screamed in pain. I'd been punched. My arms ached and my back felt like it'd been twisted into a pretzel.

The boys?

A sudden fear filled me as I twisted to look in the back. Every muscle screamed but I forced my head to move as I pushed the now floppy airbag out of the way. Austin stared back at me with wide eyes. But he looked fine.

Turning the other way I tried to find Jimmy, but he wasn't there. "Jimmy," I gasped.

"He's okay," Austin said as he unbuckled his seatbelt and helped his older brother up from the floor. I let out a long sigh when I saw that he was okay. Terrified, but okay.

"What happened?" Austin asked.

"The car," I said. "It just stopped working."

Both boys looked back at me like I'd lost my mind. Cars don't just stop working. Besides, they were male, and they knew if something had gone wrong it was my fault. Especially when it came to motor vehicles.

A thousand worries flashed through my mind. How had I screwed this up? Oh My God. What would Nanny say? I'd wrecked her car. And no way could she afford another one. A sick hopeless feeling filled me. My world sucked so much. A mom in prison. A dead father. Two little brothers who both hated the world. A sick grandmother. And we weren't even getting into my lack of a social life.

Closing my eyes, I tried to let it roll off me. All the misery of my life. Let it go, I kept

16

repeating to myself. Only after I felt a small semblance of sanity return was I able to take a deep breath and focus on the next step.

I had to push the door to get it open. It creaked and groaned, chastising me for my failure. Obviously warped from the impact. But I was able to get out and see the damage. My stomach fell. It was ruined. I didn't know anything about cars, but I knew ruined when I saw it. The front end was all smushed with water and oil dripping and running down the mountain like a small luminescence creek.

Both boys got out and stood next to me inspecting the damage. Sighing heavily, I pulled out my phone. I should probably call the cops. Isn't that what you're supposed to do after an accident? But of course, it being my phone, it was dead. I'd charged it last night but now nothing.

I stared down at my phone and shook my head then shifted to look up the highway. I'd have to flag someone down. Suddenly a cold fear began to creep up my spine. There were no cars on the road. This was I-80. Where was everyone?

We looked at each other then back up the hill then down. Nothing. There should have been a dozen cars every minute on this road.

"Where is everyone?" Jimmy asked.

"I'm hungry," Austin replied.

"You're always hungry," I snapped without looking at him. Instead, I put my hand above my eyes to block the morning sun and looked down the mountain towards Reno. This wasn't right. This quiet. The wind ruffled the ponderosa pines and grass tufts. The Truckee River rumbled a hundred yards to the right of the road. But there was nothing.

I glanced up at the sky. No airplanes. Nothing but a red-tailed hawk hovering in the distance.

"What happened?" Jimmy asked.

"I don't know," I sighed, tired of being blamed for everything that went wrong in my life. "The car was working just fine, then it wasn't."

Jimmy frowned, "I wasn't accusing, I was trying to understand. Everything is fine, then It's like the world ended. Where is everyone?"

That spine-numbing fear was spreading to the rest of my body. Suddenly I realized just how unprepared I was. I mean, we didn't even have bottled water in the car. I'd picked up a coffee that morning after we left the hotel. We were going to be home in a couple of hours. It wasn't like we were trekking through the Amazon jungle. We were driving home.

"We wait," I told them. "They always say to stay in place when things go wrong. We'll flag someone down."

The three of us sat on the untwisted part of the guardrail looking up and down the road, waiting. A gnawing fear kept chewing my stomach. Did I have enough in my account to hire a tow truck? How much do they cost? See, these are the things they don't teach you in High School. How would we survive without a car? Did Nanny have insurance? Yes, she had to.

But how long would that take? Would I be riding that monstrosity known as the school bus after spring break? God, so typical of my life. Seniors shouldn't be stuck on a school bus. It just wasn't right.

"Maybe we should walk," Jimmy said. "There was that rest stop about a mile back. There were cars there."

I was about to tell him no when the birds suddenly started screaming and taking flight and the world decided to try and throw us off. The ground dropped from beneath us like an elevator then rose up to catch us as we fell. My stomach clenched as I realized it was an earthquake, a bad one.

"Hold on," I yelled, making absolutely no sense.

The ground continued to shift and shake. Throwing me and the boys to the ground. Please, I begged. Please let us live.

Jimmy cried out in pain but before I could get to him the ground shifted again knocking me back to my knees.

He gripped his arm to his chest as he bounced up and down on the ground. I crawled over to him, my knees digging into the grit of the road as the ground continued to shake. When I got there, I pulled him into a hug then reached over and grabbed Austin, pulling him into our group.

The three of us hung onto each other as the world continued to shake and shimmy. Terrorizing us relentlessly. And then it was done. Just like that. The shaking stopped.

"Oooow," Jimmy cried as he cradled his arm.

I held my breath, terrified it was going to start again. What now? What was I supposed to do now? "Austin, are you okay?"

My littlest brother pulled away from me. Obviously embarrassed that he'd been hugged by his big sister. I wanted to yell at him to focus on what was important. But being cool is always important to young boys.

"I'm fine," he snapped as he started to whip the grit and dirt from his clothes.

"Jimmy? Anything besides the arm."

He gritted his teeth and shook his head. "I landed on it wrong. My wrist."

I gingerly tried to pry his good arm away so I could look but he refused to let me check it out. Instead grumbling under his breath and shaking his head as he turned away.

"Okay, I'll look at it in a minute." We needed to figure out what was going on. Nothing made sense anymore. Standing up, I brushed off my clothes and took a deep breath. "We're going back up to the rest area. There will be people there."

"What about our stuff," Austin asked.

Everything was packed in three separate backpacks. The kind used for schoolbooks. The boys had been responsible for their own change of clothes and any electronics. "You take Jimmy's bag," I told Austin.

"Why me?" He whined.

"Because I said so," I snapped then immediately regretted it. But Austin grabbed his brother's bag.

"Do you want to let me look at your arm?" I asked Jimmy. He gritted his teeth and shook his head.

Fine, he'd let me do it when he was ready. "Come on," I said as I started back up the mountain. Within a dozen steps, I was second-guessing my decision. It was going to be a long walk uphill.

Bending at the waist, I ignored the pain in my calves and focused on putting one foot in front of the other. We were about a half mile into our trip when we rounded a bend to discover an SUV parked in the middle of the road. On the other side of the road, headed up the mountain.

My heart jumped. People. Then fell when we discovered it was empty. How had they avoided getting into a crash? Maybe it really had been my fault. Where had they gone? Maybe the rest stop. And why had they stopped in the middle of the road?

Shifting my pack, I started up the mountain knowing the boys would follow. "Just get me," there, I swore under my breath. I couldn't stop thinking about sitting at a picnic table and resting my head on my arms. I was going to spend ten minutes pretending the universe wasn't out to get me.

"There," Austin said.

I looked up and was rewarded with the beautiful sight of a modern rest stop. Restrooms. Picnic tables. A drinking fountain. A sign explaining how lumber had been cut in that area for the mines in Virginia City during the gold rush.

But I was focused on the people. Or the lack of them. The only person was a big man sitting on the curb next to his big motorcycle.

Two cars, a sedan and a pickup truck, were parked in the lot, but empty.

I glanced over at the biker guy and tried to steer the boys around him. I needed the bathroom bad. Of course, there was no power. The bathroom was dark except for a faint light coming in from a vent. I shuddered but a girl has got to do what a girl has got to do.

When I came back out, I quickly rounded up the boys and herded them towards a picnic bench.

"This isn't right," James said, still cradling his injured arm. "Cars aren't working. No power. Something happened."

"OOOOH," Austin mocked, "It's the end of the world and Jimmy thinks he's Will Smith in I am Legend."

I was about to chastise him when the motorcycle guy suddenly stood up and began marching up the road back to Truckee. Not a word to us. No explanation. No questions. And suddenly I realized how bad things were. The guy was abandoning his motorcycle. I began to realize just how alone we were.

I could tell that Jimmy could see it also. No food, no people. We were so in trouble when Austin gasped and pointed over my shoulder. I turned to see a boy about my age stepping out of the forest like he owned the world.

He nodded towards us then adjusted his huge backpack and turned downhill. Tall, with wide shoulders. A stubbly beard. A green flannel shirt, jeans, and hiking boots. A suede jacket tied across the top of his pack. The guy looked like he'd spent the last two weeks in the wilderness and enjoyed every minute of it.

"Hey," I yelled, jumping up and rushing after him.

He stopped and turned, and I'll admit, I sort of froze. What was I going to say? Um, can you tell us what is going on? "Something happened," I managed to say. "We were in an accident."

Letting out a long breath he looked at each of us then down the mountain. "The world just ended. Everything you thought you knew is wrong as of two hours ago."

I stared back at him and deep in my insides I knew he was right.

Chapter Three

<u>Chase</u>

There is something about a pretty girl needing help that pulls at a guy's soul. Auburn hair held back by a barrette, large green eyes, an angelic face, and all the right curves in all the right places. Yes, most definitely the kind of girl who deserved a knight in shining armor.

Unfortunately for her. Not my job. I needed to get to Idaho. I could see it all laid out. These people were going to slow me down. But like I said, something in the way she looked made me stop. I knew I was making a mistake but stopped anyway.

"What happened?" She asked then looked at the two younger boys. Obviously, her brothers.

"An asteroid hit us. A big one. In the Pacific. Set off an EMP."

She looked confused but the older boy gasped. He'd obviously read the same books I had growing up.

"A what?" she asked.

"EMP," her brother said. "An Electro Magnetic Pulse. It knocks out all electrical things. Anything with a transistor."

Her brow furrowed even further. "For how long?"

"Forever," I told her, "Until we build it all out again, so at least twenty years or so."

The color drained from her face as she began to understand. "That's what happened to Nanny's car. All the cars."

I nodded. The girl wasn't dumb.

"So … What do we do?"

This is where my gut told me to not get involved. Their problems were not my problems. So I said, "You might think about going up to Truckee. They've got cops, people, food."

She stared at me trying to understand then shook her head. "No, our grandmother needs us. She lives in Reno."

I shrugged, "Your call. I'm walking to Reno then Idaho. You're welcome to tag along. But I set a good pace."

A doubt filled her eyes. She was easy to read. A strange boy, no authorities, the world just ended. Maybe it wouldn't be too smart to go with me. Which was perfectly understandable in my book. But I thought about my sister Haley, and my cousin Cassie. What if they were all alone on the road? A cold shiver shot down my spine.

Taking a deep breath, I said, "Listen, in all honesty, I'm probably your best bet. My uncle would kill me if I was ever anything but a gentleman."

Still, the doubt remained when the older boy said, "We need to go with him."

I looked at the boy trying to understand why he thought so when I noticed him holding his arm to his chest.

"What happened?" I asked, nodding at his arm.

He shrugged, "I fell on it wrong during the earthquake."

Nodding, I reached out and told him to squeeze my fingers. The girl shot me an angry look then gawked when the boy complied by squeezing my two fingers, wincing in pain. I pushed and prodded. The wrist was swollen and stiff, but I would guess not broken.

"It might be broken, but if it is, it's only a hairline."

"We don't have any first aid stuff," the girl said.

"Neither do I," I replied as I lowered my pack and removed my least favorite AC/DC T-shirt. I pulled my buck knife out of its sheath and flipped it open then cut one long continuous strip three inches wide.

Both boys studied my knife with obvious want. I could tell right away they didn't have a man in their life, or they'd already have a knife.

"Here," I said as I gingerly began to wrap the boy's wrist in a figure eight. "Let me

28

know if it swells more. We don't want to cut off circulation."

The boy nodded as he flexed his fingers.

I cut the last long strip of cloth and tied it around his neck and helped him slip his arm into the sling. "It's the best I can do for now."

"We'll get it X-rayed when we get home," the girl said.

Scoffing, I shook my head as I lifted my pack. "X-ray machines don't work anymore."

Her jaw dropped as the reality was beginning to sink in.

"I'm Chase Conrad, by the way."

She hesitated then replied, "Meagan Foster, these are my brothers Jimmy and Austin."

"James," Jimmy said, correcting her. I almost smiled. An Eleven-year-old boy who wanted desperately to be thought of as older. Of course he did.

"Okay, we need to get going. It's forty miles to Reno."

All three of them blanched for a second but they shouldered their school-type packs and we started down the road. I had to remind myself not to go too fast and held back as I tried to figure out what I was going to do with these three.

Just get them to Reno, I told myself. Turn them over to their people then hit the road.

Fifteen minutes later, we passed their car, She'd scrunched it pretty bad.

"How much does a tow truck cost?" she asked out of the blue.

I laughed. "Nowadays they are priceless. There are no tow trucks anymore."

Taking a deep breath she nodded, but I think it really hadn't settled in yet. That took another ten minutes. When we found the dead guy behind the wheel of his Buick. Stuck in the middle of the road I noticed that gray pallor and held my arm out to stop them getting any closer.

Meagan ignored me and pushed past only to freeze when she realized what was going on.

"A pacemaker, I'd bet," I said.

Meagan stared at the guy then back at me like she expected me to fix things. "What should we do?"

I didn't laugh I just shrugged then started for Reno.

"Hey, wait," she called as she hurried to catch up with me. "You can't just leave him there."

"Why not?" I asked. "There are going to be hundreds, thousands. We can't bury them all. We don't have time."

Her brow furrowed as she stared at me like I was a monster, but I let it run off my back. Idaho, I kept telling myself. What this girl thought of me didn't matter.

"He's right," James said as he passed his sister and fell in next to me.

I glanced over then shrugged to get my pack to sit better. Meagan fell in on the other side of her brother. The younger one, Austin, scooted in next to her. The four of us walked down the middle of the road. Twice more we passed empty cars. The people deciding to walk home.

A noise up ahead set my nerves to full alert. Sure enough, when we rounded a bend there were a dozen people surrounding a four-car pile up. The body of an old man lay on the pavement. Two more sat next to the guard rail, a lady holding a bloody cloth to her head.

"Keep walking," I hissed under my breath.

"But ..." Meagan started but she bit her tongue and kept quiet as we passed through the group of people and kept walking down the hill.

"Why?" she demanded. "Why couldn't we stop."

31

Letting out a long breath I stopped myself from snapping at her and instead said. "Because if we take too long, we will end up camping there, with all those people and I don't have enough food to feed them."

She hesitated as she began to work it out.

"As it is, we'll have to camp along the way. I figured just this side of Floristan."

"Why don't we stop there? Do they have a motel?"

I laughed. "If they do it will be full. Besides, I don't want to get caught in a town after dark. People are going to be jumpy, to say the least."

She frowned, "But we can't camp. We don't have the stuff, tent, sleeping bags."

"One night won't kill you. But hey, I'm not in charge of you. You do what you want. Me? I'm camping down by the river."

James used his good hand to pull her down and whisper something to her. I ignored them as we approached a semi-truck jack-knifed across the road. We had to work our way onto the median to get past it. The Driver sat up in the cab, the door open, picking his teeth with a toothpick.

I nodded to him, but kept moving. He studied us for a minute, his eyes lingering on Meagan for too long then back to me, evaluating. I made sure to look him in the eye, letting him know I knew what he was thinking and I wasn't going to let anything happen to the girl.

He got my message and simply shrugged then swung his legs back into the cab before leaning back.

"Too many people are taking too long to figure it out," I said when we got past the truck. "I swear they are all waiting for someone else to come fix things. For the authorities to tell them what to do."

"Can you blame them?" Meagan asked.

"People are going to be dying over the next few months. And then it is going to get real bad. The people who take the right actions now, just maybe, might make it."

The color drained from her face.

"What should we be doing?" James asked.

"Water, Food, Shelter. Enough to last through next winter."

"But? ... How?" Meagan muttered.

I let out a long breath. "The people who figure it out live. The ones that don't, don't."

There was a long pause then she shook her head. "You're just trying to scare us. I don't know why. Maybe you think it's funny, scaring women and kids. But it can't be that bad."

Slamming to a stop I turned to stare at her, my brow furrowing. "Think it through. No electricity. No vehicles. Maybe ancient ones, from the seventies, they might work. But the gas pumps need electricity. And even if you siphon it from the tanks. It's going to run out eventually.

"How much food do you think there is in a town like Reno? Two weeks maybe. Don't forget you've got a big chunk of tourists. So I'd say one week, maybe ten days. And no more is coming in. Think about the truck we passed. All the food is stuck in warehouses or on the road."

"But ..." she stammered. "Come on. The government must have known this might happen."

Here I laughed. "Knowing is one thing. Doing something about it, too expensive for something that might not happen."

She continued to stare at me as her eyes grew misty. My heart broke seeing the sadness in her eyes. But there was nothing I could do about it except get them to their home then they were someone else's problem.

Chapter Four

<u>Meagan</u>

How was this possible? I mean any of it. I swear it was like being in some weird dream where nothing made sense. I was walking down the middle of a freeway with a strange boy.

Who was he? I wondered for the thousandth time. I mean he steps out of the forest like Robin Hood. Big, strong, competent, and confident. Have I told you how confident Chase Conrad was? Almost arrogant.

I knew the type from school. Jocks usually, their size, athletic ability gave them status that gave them confidence. But there was something different about this boy. Oh, I'm sure he was the star of every sport in his school. But there was more. The whole loner thing about backpacking through the mountains all alone.

Or maybe it was the way he interacted with Jimmy. No judgment, no power plays. Jimmy had picked it up immediately and responded.

But still. What did I know about him? Obviously. I mean, he could be an ax murderer. He even had his own axe tied to his backpack.

Letting out a long breath, I rolled my eyes at myself. Here I was dealing with the end of the world and I was trying to figure out a strange boy who was going to disappear as soon as we got home.

Focus, I told myself. First off, it couldn't be as bad as he said. Yes, sure, for right now, here it was a natural disaster. But FEMA would come in, the army. Food to last through next winter. Don't be ridiculous. This country produced so much food we gave it away for free.

As we walked, Chase started to pull ahead then made himself slow down to let us catch up. I knew it was bothering him, our slowness, but tough, we weren't keeping him. We could find Reno on our own.

Twice we passed more people. Every time Chase insisted we not stop. I think because we were so young they didn't look to us for answers. In fact, us moving through them was appreciated. One less problem for them to deal with.

We were a few hours into our long walk when Chase pointed to the shade under a big pine. "Let's take a break," he said as he pulled his canteen strap up and over his shoulder and offered it to me. I took a long sip then passed it to my brothers.

"First rule," Chase said, "No water unless it has been boiled or treated with chlorine."

"What about at home," Austin asked as he passed the canteen back to Chase.

"I wouldn't trust the water treatment facility. The wrong bug could wipe out half the town."

I studied Chase and realized he was trying to teach us things before he left us. It was up to us whether we followed his advice, but at least we would know. A small part deep inside of me appreciated it, but another part told me it was going to be hard without someone like Chase in our lives.

What did I know about survival? Nothing. I mean nothing. Nanny didn't preserve food. We didn't have a garden.

"Rule Two," Chase said, addressing both boys. "Don't trust anyone except family."

"What about you," I said. "You're not family."

He studied me then shook his head. "You'd be an idiot to trust me. Or any stranger. You're okay for now. Things haven't gotten real bad yet."

I scoffed, dead guys sitting in cars wasn't real bad? As if seeing my doubt he said, "Think about a month from now. People are down to one meal a day if they are lucky. Their kids are starving to death. You have something that they need. Believe me, they are going to try and take it.

"Oh, come on," I said. "People aren't like that. After every natural disaster people work together to get things going again."

He laughed and shook his head before smiling at Jimmy and lifting an eyebrow, obviously dismissing me as a silly girl.

An anger flashed inside of me how dare he treat me like that? He had no idea about me and what I had gone through these last two years. Clenching my teeth I was about to tell him we didn't need his help when he said. "You're naivety is going to get your brothers killed."

That was it, no way was I putting up with this, grabbing Austin's arm I started to push him back onto the road. "Let's go guys."

Jimmy said, "Meagan, don't be stupid."

Glaring at my brother I was about to yell at him when a movement uphill caught my eye, looking over my shoulder a new nervousness filled me. Five men were walking down the road towards us. The truck driver was one of them. I could still remember the skanky chill that ran down my back when he looked at me.

Suddenly, Chase dropped his backpack and stepped up next to me. "Stay here. In fact, get back by the tree."

"Why?" I asked.

He took a deep breath then looked at me and said, "Because if you have to run, you'll have a head start."

More of his dramatic fear-mongering I thought as I made a point of staying right where I was at, watching the men approach. They were each in their mid-forties. Dressed in everything from jeans to business suits. One with a well-trimmed beard. Nothing that said they were a group except that they were all walking in the same direction.

My heart hitched when they turned towards us. I felt Chase tense up as he instinctively moved between the men and my brothers.

The men kept approaching, studying us when the bearded one said, "You got any food?"

Chase simply shook his head and said, "No."

Three of the men hesitated but bearded guy kept coming, saying, "I don't believe you. Let's check out your pack."

It was so fast that I gasped. Chase pulled his buck knife and flicked his wrist. The five-inch silver blade snapped into position before anyone knew what was happening. "Again," Chase said, "No."

All five men stopped. I could see it in their minds. They had thought we were easy targets. And they wouldn't have been wrong if Chase wasn't with us. But now here was a boy unwilling to back down. Ready to fight for what was his.

My heart pounded in my chest as I held my breath, terrified. There were five of them.

"You can't take us all," The truck driver said then he turned and stared at me, running his eyes up over my body sending a nervous chill down my spine.

Chase spit into the ground. "I don't need to kill all five of you. Just two. The other three will back off and leave us alone. Who wants to be first?"

I swear it was like an old-time western and Chase was staring down the outlaws.

The five men continued to glare at Chase. I could see the anger in their eyes. They hated being thwarted by a boy. But I think they were coming to realize that Chase wasn't a boy. They'd run into a hard man who wasn't going to back down.

I glanced over at him and felt something shift inside of me. He reminded me of a guard dog protecting its flock. There was that story out last year about a pack of coyotes coming onto a ranch and trying to get into a flock of goats. The guard dog chased them down and killed nine of them.

That was Chase. These men didn't know what they were getting into.

Thankfully, one of the men. An older one in a business suit pulled at the bearded guy and said, "Come on. It's not worth it. If he's got anything it won't be much."

Truck driver guy stared at me with cold eyes and said, "He's got something all right. Something I want."

A cold fear filled my heart. I am girl enough to know fear. But this was different. A cold, calculated desire out in the open. Of course, I realized. There was nothing to stop him. Nothing but Chase Conrad.

Chase let out a long breath. "Are you guys really going to attack a bunch of kids? I mean, what would your families think of you?"

A guilty look passed through them then like a flock of birds reacting together, they all turned and started down the road without speaking to each other.

Chase stood there, his knife out ready, not moving until they rounded a bend down the hill.

"Third rule," he said to Jimmy. "Always carry a gun."

"You were able to keep them away without a gun," I said. I hated guns. Mom had used a gun to kill my dad.

Chase just shook his head. "I was able to scare them away because they didn't have a gun. If they had they'd have shot me and taken what they wanted. Especially that truck driver."

A cold chill shot down my spine as I realized he was right.

"Come on," he said as he shouldered his huge pack then began walking off the highway down to the river.

We hurried to catch up. "Where are you going?" I demanded. We'd spent most of the day walking downhill and now he was headed back up.

"I want to give them some room and it gets dark early around here because of the mountains. We need to find a place to camp."

"Do you have a tent big enough for all of us?

Chase shook his head. "I just sleep under the stars. If it rains, I throw my jacket over my face and burrow down into my bag."

Suddenly a new fear filled my stomach. We were going to be sleeping outside, in the dark, with a strange boy. Austin shot me a look then reached over and took my hand. I didn't know if he was seeking comfort or giving it.

Chase of course was a wizard in the wilderness. He found a spot next to the river with a six-foot bluff where the river had worn into the hillside. He had the boys gather firewood then made them go get three times more. "It's going to be a long night and I want to scare the coyotes, bears, and mountain lions."

"There are grizzly bears around here?" Austin asked.

Chase shook his head as he kneeled next to the fire to stir the coals. "Black bears. The last grizzly was killed a hundred years ago."

I felt useless as I looked around and realized how much I didn't know. We passed through here in our cars and had no idea what was really around us. "What can I do to help?" I asked, suddenly desperate for something to keep me busy.

Chase pulled out two small pots and told me to fill them with water from the river and boil them. "Throw a handful of rice into one of them." He then removed a small fishing rod and extended it out to full length, gave Jimmy a quick smile, and walked to the bank. Within ten minutes he had three good-sized trout on the bank.

All I could do was stare. He made it look too easy. He caught my look and said, "Years of practice."

The four of us sat around the fire, passed the rice around, and ate trout while the sky turned into night. The stars filled every inch of the sky as a weird, detached feeling filled me. It could have been a thousand years ago. People sitting around a campfire, their bellies full of freshly caught fish.

But, a long day caught up to us and I couldn't stop yawning. Chase chuckled then broke out his sleeping bag, unzipping it to full open. "Backs to the bluff."

"Jimmy take that end," I said. "I'll take the middle. Austin here." The boys shrugged but they didn't realize I wanted a brother between me and Chase Conrad. I'd have been bothered by nervous energy all night if I tried to sleep next to Chase.

I needn't have worried. Chase got his leather suede coat with the wool collar and sat by the fire all night, feeding it sticks, occasionally getting up to check out our surroundings. I knew he was making sure none of those men came back.

As I fell asleep, I sent up a silent thank you that it had been Chase who approached us. Things could have been so much worse. As we would soon learn.

Chapter Five

Chase

The night sky was turning purple when I kicked dirt over the fire. We needed to get going. Taking a deep breath I glanced at my three charges. God, I'd never known such innocents. They were clueless. Not only the wilderness. But what was coming?

The James kid wanted to learn and did the best he could with an injured arm. Austin was too quiet and stuck too close to his sister. The boy needed to be pushed.

As for Miss Meagan Foster. She looked so sweet with the sleeping bag pulled up to her chin, a wisp of hair blowing in the wind. Careful, I reminded myself. A girl in distress was just too tempting. Besides, I needed to get to Idaho.

Meagan opened her eyes to find me staring at her. I smiled and turned to give her some privacy.

"You put the fire out."

"We need to be going," I answered. "I need to get you to your home. If I'm lucky I can put five miles on the road after I drop you guys off."

Her brow furrowed for some reason but then she woke her brothers and helped them roll up my bag. We were on the road fifteen minutes later.

46

"What about breakfast," Austin asked.

"You won't die. Besides, skipping meals is good for you. It builds character."

Meagan shot me a bewildered look. "You don't believe that do you."

I laughed. "No, but it makes having an empty stomach easier to put up with."

When we got back up on the road, I let out a long sigh. The reason I wanted to get going was I figured everyone would still be asleep. We could get miles under our feet without being bothered. Unfortunately, the first group of people we encountered were hovering around a campfire, staring at us as we walked by.

I quickly examined them to confirm none of the five men from yesterday were with the bunch. Four adults and three kids, the youngest maybe five. My heart went out to them. "Nobody is coming," I told them.

"You don't know that," The bigger of the men snapped.

I shrugged then asked, "You seen any cars? This is a major highway and there hasn't been a car through here in a day. Why?"

A heavy silence fell over the group. I ignored it and kept moving forward. I'd done the best I could. I couldn't save everyone. Especially those too dumb to see the truth.

We took a break a couple hours in. Four times we'd passed people sleeping in their cars. And we probably passed two dozen empty cars. Two of them were wrapped around guard rails and a third in a ditch.

Finally, we moved out of the sparse forests and onto the dry desert grassland. We crossed over into Nevada and then passed through the small town of Verde. I was tempted to stop at a small grocery store but the guy standing in the front door with a shotgun killed that idea. Instead, I kept them moving.

The mountains became desert as the Reno skyline came into view. Just get them home. I kept telling myself. I could be back out of town before nightfall. I did not want to be caught in the city after dark.

We kept to the highway, passing housing divisions, the newer, nicer ones the farther from town. The silence was eerie. No air conditioning units, no distant sirens, nothing but a morning dove cooing.

A sick feeling filled my gut when I saw all these people and no electricity, no vehicles. What were they going to do in a couple of weeks?

"There," James said, pointing to a subdivision. Just like any other, middle, middle class. Older. With three-bedroom ranch houses that looked like they'd been built in the eighties back when Reno was going to be the next Las Vegas.

"Nanny will be so happy to see us," Meagan said as we turned down an off-ramp.

A cold dread filled me when I saw the people staring at us as we walked down their street. These were their neighbors, but the look of worry and questions wouldn't stop rubbing against me.

Competition, I realized. That was what we were. I think people were beginning to understand just how much trouble they were in. Maybe not intellectually, not yet. But definitely, emotionally, they knew.

"That's ours," Meagan said as she pointed to a typical ranch. Brown grass out front. A big plastic trashcan on the curb, Rushing past me, Meagan opened the front door and yelled, "Nanny, we're here."

"Meagan," A weak voice called from in back.

Both boys raced past me and into the house.

I held back at the door. I hadn't been invited in. I just needed to know they were okay then I could hit the road. Maybe they'd let me top off my water. The house smelled of old air and I realized that without air conditioning it'd get stuffy real fast.

Suddenly Meagan yelled, "Chase,"

49

I dropped my pack and rushed in then turned right to find her next to an older woman lying on the carpet. Meagan looked up at me with fear in her eyes as she slid an arm behind the woman's back and tried to help her up.

"Stop," I said as I put a restraining hand on Meagan's arm. "What happened?"

"She fell," Meagan snapped. "We need to get her to her bed."

I continued to hold Meagan's arm back before she could do any damage, "Mrs. Foster?"

The old woman looked back at me, slightly confused but she nodded then looked to Meagan for an explanation.

"This is Chase, Nanny. He helped us get home. Everything ... I wrecked the car. I ..."

"When did you fall," I asked the older woman.

"Yesterday," she said with a weak voice. My heart hurt thinking about the woman stuck here on the floor. No family. No working phone. No one to help. "Where does it hurt."

The woman scoffed, "Where doesn't it is a better question."

I took a deep breath then pulled my canteen off my hip and unscrewed the top before holding it to her lips. "Here, drink this, it will help."

The woman studied me for a long moment then said, "What, is it magical? Is it going to make my legs work again?"

"It's just water," I said then let out my breath as she took a long drink.

"Okay," I said to the boys, "James, open the door to her room. Austin stand back, be ready to help." I then pushed Meghan out of the way so I could get behind Mrs. Foster. "I'm going to lift you up. Do you think if we get your feet under you, you can stand?"

She took a deep breath then nodded. I bent at my knees and lifted her. As I lifted, I could feel how frail she was. I swear her bones felt like bird bones, lighter than they looked. But I got her up. Meghan held out her hands ready to catch her if she dropped.

Somehow, we got her into her room and onto her bed. I left Meagan to care for her as I hustled the boys out of the room.

James gave me a quick tour. I pushed aside my manners and pulled open the refrigerator then the cupboards to check out their food situation. My heart sank. Maybe a week's worth. Grinding my teeth I tried not to let the boys see how disappointed I was.

A week? But really, I couldn't be critical. They were typical. I was staring into a pretty barren backyard when Meghan found me and said, "Nanny wants to talk to you. I've told her what happened. She said she thought it might be something like that."

"Why does she want to talk to me?"

Meagan shrugged. "I told her you were in a hurry. That you needed to get to your family in Idaho."

I nodded, the least I could do was talk to the woman. I knocked at her door then entered when she told me to. The room smelled of Lavender and the sharp tang of Vicks Vapor Rub. A nice room with a dresser with family pictures. Each of her grandchildren. A young man. And an old black and white picture of a guy in a uniform.

"Mrs. Foster," I said. "Meagan said you wanted to see me."

The woman was sitting up in her bed, her blanket over her lap. She looked past me at Meagan and said, "That's okay dear. You go make sure the boys are settled."

Meagan's brow narrowed as she looked at her grandmother then at me. I shrugged.

Once Meagan had closed the door behind her, the old woman patted the side of the bed for me to sit down. "I need you closer, hurts my neck to look up. And you're too tall."

I laughed to myself and shrugged before sitting down. The woman studied me for a long moment then said, "Thank you for getting my grandchildren home to me."

I nodded, what could I say? "It wasn't that big a deal."

The woman shook her head, "You are a terrible liar."

Laughing, I said, "My sister has told me that more than once."

The woman took my hand then said. "I am dying."

My heart fell as I saw the certainty in her eyes.

She continued. "I had a heart operation last year. My medicine will run out next week. That and I've got diabetes, take insulin four times a day. Thrombosis in the legs, and oh yeah, my Kidneys are shutting down."

My jaw dropped as I desperately tried to figure out what to say.

"The docs said I might live six months. But that was with the medicine and the last bit in the hospital. Now. Two weeks, tops."

"You don't know," I said, unwilling to admit the obvious.

She smiled then patted my hand. "The kids, they don't know."

My heart fell when I thought about Meagan and the two boys discovering the truth. Or worse, discovering their dead grandmother.

"What can I do?" I asked.

She smiled then said, "I need a promise. A promise to a dying woman. A promise that can't be broken."

I hesitated as I looked at the woman. Deep down I knew where this was leading and was trying to figure a way out.

She nodded, seeing the understanding in my eyes. "I need you to promise to take care of my grandchildren. Can you do that?"

"Um ..."

"I can die content knowing they'll be taken care of. My biggest fear was leaving them all alone in this world. Normal times would have been bad enough. But the authorities would have done something. They wouldn't have starved. Now? But with you, they will have a chance."

I hemmed and hawed, unwilling to say the words that would trap me.

"Please," she begged as her frail fingers gripped my hand. "Please help me die in peace."

I looked into her eyes and thought of my mother. She would be furious at me for even hesitating. Sighing, I nodded. "I promise to take care of your grandchildren."

The woman sighed as she closed her eyes and slumped onto the pillows. I gently placed her hand next to her then backed out.

"What did she want?" Meagan asked as I quietly closed the door behind me.

I was tempted to tell her everything. That her grandmother had finessed a dying promise from me. But I saw the love she had for the older woman and simply shrugged. "She asked me to hang around for a couple of days until she is feeling better.

Meagan studied me for a long moment then asked, "What did you tell her?"

"I told her I'd help out for a bit but then I was headed up north."

She frowned as she tried to take it all in then she said. "I think she is dying. But I don't have the heart to tell her." Then somehow, she was in my arms, crying on my chest. I did what any sane man would do. I put my arms around her and let her know that everything would be okay.

Wow, was I wrong on that one.

Chapter Six

Meagan

I clung to Chase like he was a lifeline. My world was dissolving around me, and he was the only thing I knew I could rely on. Two days together and I just knew I could depend upon him I had been terrified that he was going to disappear. But now, he was staying at least for a few days. Long enough for us to figure out what to do. A sense of relief flowed through me as I began to understand just how terrified I was about him leaving.

Suddenly realizing how ridiculous I was being, I pulled away and wiped at my eyes. "I'm sorry," I said, unable to look up into his eyes. I didn't want to see disappointment or worse, disapproval. Turning away, I called the boys.

Once they joined us, I put my arm around their shoulders then asked Chase, "What next? What should we do?"

His brow furrowed and I could see his mind working a million miles a minute. There was so much that needed to be done. Finally, he let out a long breath. "Rule four. Always have a way to make light. Candles, oil lamps, matches, or a Bic lighter?"

"There are two candles in the kitchen drawer. Big white ones," I said.

Chase lowered his head in defeat and shook it slowly. "That's it? No oil lamps. Just two candles."

"I've got a flashlight," Austin said then added with a frown. "I just need to find batteries."

Chase sighed. "Okay. One candle to be lit at dark and placed on the coffee table. You'll sleep in your rooms without any candles."

"And," I asked.

"Tuna," he said. "I saw some cans. The Mayo in the refrigerator is still good. You make a ton of sandwiches while we gather firewood. Tomorrow we're going to cook all the meat in the freezer before it goes bad."

That night, the house was so quiet I swear I could hear the walls breathe. Chase crashed on our couch. Nanny was still not up out of bed. My heart was filled with worry but I couldn't stop thinking about the boy out in our living room and what were we going to do to survive.

The next morning I began to find out. We spent the morning cutting long strips off roasts and drying them over a smoky fire Chase built on the patio. Chase and the boys broke up the dining room chairs for firewood. Then the table. He rigged up some kind of blanket thing that kept the smoke in.

Once the meat was dried out like leather Chase had me wrap it in plastic wrap, then aluminum foil, then into plastic bags. "It will keep for a month at least," he told me.

Unfortunately, there was a hint of varnish taste on the meat. But I was pretty sure we weren't going to mind in a couple of weeks.

Chase put a pot of rice on the grate over the fire then stepped back pushing at his lower back. "We can stretch things to ten days," he said. "But we're going to need food soon. I've checked, you guys don't have anything worth trading. No booze, no hard drugs. We're going to have to beg, borrow, or steal.

I swallowed hard as I began to see what he was always going on about. Before the world ended, I never really thought about our food. You got it from the store. Nanny paid for it. Oh, sure, we didn't get fancy stuff. No steaks, generic brands whenever possible. But no one ever went hungry. Not in America.

It wasn't just me. My brothers were beginning to understand. Austin had become clingy, refusing to let me out of his sight. Jimmy had become sullen, not talking just staring out the back sliding glass door at Chase maintaining the fire.

They were worried. I knew that look. I'd seen it a lot over the last two years. A father killed by their mother will put a desperate fear into a person. What if I became like her? Will she try to kill me if I upset her? Why didn't I stop her? Is there something wrong with me that I let her do that? I know the boys had those thoughts because I had them on a permanent basis.

Suddenly there was a flash of light then a heavy boom rocked the whole house. My immediate thought was another asteroid.

"Meagan!" Nanny yelled from her room. I was still trying to figure it out when it happened again then a third time. Then the skies opened up. A torrential rain pounded the ground like a gazillion hammers hitting an anvil.

Chase hurried in sliding the door closed just as another boom echoed through the house.

We all stared in amazement as the rain whipped back and forth, pounding the windows and shaking the house.

"Meagan," Nanny yelled again.

"We're fine," I yelled back as I hurried down the hall to her room. The house had grown dark and gloomy in the middle of the afternoon. "It's just a thunderstorm," I told her.

She let out a long breath then closed her eyes. My heart hitched when I saw how pale she had gotten. I would have called 911 or taken her to a hospital myself. But one, the phones didn't work. And oh yeah, I didn't have a car anymore. And finally, the world as we knew it was gone. I doubted the hospital could do anything for her. Not without electricity.

Once she was sleeping I went back to the living room to find all three boys standing by the glass door looking out.

"What are you doing, get away from there," I snapped at them.

All three of them looked back at me like I'd just ruined their fun. But Chase finally nodded and tapped them on the shoulder to move them back. We moved to the far end of the living room to the couch and sat quietly.

"I've never seen it this bad," I said.

"The asteroid," Chase said. "It must have thrown half the ocean up into the air. Some of it is coming down on Reno Nevada. The rest will be tidal waves the size of skyscrapers."

"I thought they were supposed to knock it off course," Jimmy said. "We were talking about it at school."

Chase let out a long breath, "According to my uncle who was visiting JPL, they ended up slowing it down which put it in line with Earth. And they didn't have time for a second shot."

"What about Mom?" Austin asked. "She's in California."

Chase glanced at me with raised eyebrows obviously asking me to explain why my mom was there and not here with us. My stomach froze into a knot. No way was I telling him the truth. Instead, I put an arm around Austin and pulled him into a hug. "She will be fine. She's a hundred miles from the ocean."

I could see Chase's curiosity, but another thunderclap rocked the house pulling our attention back to the storm raging outside.

We watched the storm until it got too dark to see. But the steady patter on the windows interrupted by the occasional thunder let us know it was still there. I finally got the boys off to bed, checked on Nanny, then returned to sit on the couch next to Chase.

A weird awkwardness filled the air as I realized we were all alone with a single dancing candle flame the only light. In any other situation, it would have been romantic.

"What other things should we be doing?" I asked him just to break the tension.

He frowned for a moment then said, "The basics, Water, Food, Shelter. Today, tomorrow, long term. It's the long term that is going to be hard. Reno isn't known for being surrounded by farms. A few ranches, but not much more. All the food has to come in from the outside. That is a lot of people to feed. And you saw, nothing is moving."

A sick feeling settled at the bottom of my stomach.

"You don't have the setup to start a garden," he continued. "And you don't have the time. Plus. If you did, people would just come and take it."

He was serious. I could see it, he really did think people were evil. I almost laughed in his face. Believe me, I understood some people could be evil. I was related to one by birth. But not most. I had to hope most people were good or what was the point?

"You're grandmother doesn't have a gun. Does she?" he asked hopefully.

I bit my lip while I shook my head as I realized. Three days ago I would have told him no, even if she did have one. But not now. Now I could see where a gun might come in handy. Might! But we were a gun-free house.

Don't forget, my mother had used a gun to kill my father.

Chase let out a long breath then shook his head before he closed his eyes and leaned back. "We'll have to get one somewhere. We're not walking all the way to Idaho without one."

"We?" I gasped.

He just tilted his head and looked at me like I was a lost puppy for not seeing the truth.

"We can't stay here. We won't survive."

"No," I said with my best emphatic tone as I shook my head. "If you have to go. Then go. We will be just fine."

He actually rolled his eyes at me then said. "No, you won't. You've got enough food for ten days. What then?"

"I don't know. But we will figure it out. Like I said, no one is making you stay."

He scoffed then said, "Your grandmother is. She made me promise to stay until she dies, then I can take you."

"What?" I yelled as I stood up to get away from him. How could he be so cold? So crass. He was talking about my grandmother as if she was just another statistic."

"Meagan," he said as he let out a long breath. "The world has changed. People who can't face reality are going to end up dead. Even those that can are still going to end up dead. Deep down. You know your grandmother is going to die. Even if we could get her to a hospital, they won't have electricity. No machines for dialysis. Her Insulin is going to run out. You need to prepare yourself."

I stared at him, unable to accept his words while knowing deep down that he was right. "We are not walking to Idaho."

He studied me for a long moment then said, "We'll talk about it later. When … Later."

I knew he was just kicking the issue down the road. But I didn't want to face this new reality. If I lost Nanny, I would have lost my last rock. The one person I had always known loved me. The one person who would put my needs above her own. If she died. That left me in charge. In charge at the end of the world.

A sick feeling filled me. I didn't want to have to make decisions. Unfortunately, I feared I would be making all of them very soon.

Chapter Seven

<u>Chase</u>

It rained for two days. Not a gentle mist. No, a heavy downpour that threatened to flood the house. We ended up putting rolled-up blankets along the bottom of the sliding glass door. They kept out most of the water. The street out front was like a small river with six inches of fast-moving water rushing towards the Truckee.

I spent the time climbing the walls. I was trapped inside with oblivious people. No supplies, or very little. No weapons. And no idea what they were facing. Plus I had to find things to keep them busy. God, I hate busy work. But I didn't need them bugging out over things. I needed their hands busy.

I told the boys to figure out a way to build bows and arrows. I didn't care if they were any good. I just wanted them to stop asking me questions.

I had Meagan inventory every bit of food, medicine, and tools. Again, it wasn't important, but it kept her busy.

On the third morning, I woke to a silvery gray sky but no rain. Throwing the blankets back I jumped off the couch and made a quick trip to the restroom saying a silent thank you that the water still worked. How much longer? Was the system gravity-fed? Or were we just running on stuff in the pipes?

And how long was it safe? With all this rain I'd bet the system had been flooded somewhere mixing sewage with fresh water.

When I got back to the kitchen, I separated five pieces of beef jerky and five bowls of leftover rice, a cup each. That would be it until dinner.

Meagan came in rubbing her eyes. I had to hold back a gawking smile. The girl was adorable in butterfly fleece pajamas, her hair all messed up. She frowned at me then looked out to see the rain had stopped.

We ate our breakfast in awkward silence. "I'm going out to look for food," I told her after the last bite.

"Give me a second. I'll go too."

"No," I said, shaking my head.

Her brow furrowed then she sighed. "Listen, Chase. I realize you know more about this stuff than I do. But you are not in charge of me. I will go where I want when I want."

I stared back at her wondering if I should put my foot down. But I realized she was right. I couldn't stop her. Besides, maybe she would begin to see how bad it really was. "Ten minutes."

"Why so early?"

"Murderers and rapists sleep in. We might be able to avoid them. If we're lucky."

Her jaw dropped as she stared at me. "You're serious, aren't you? You really think like that."

"Humor me," I told her. "Chalk it up to a rough childhood."

She scoffed as she turned away and mumbled something about me not knowing what rough was. While waiting, I emptied my pack except for the hatchet. Meagan woke up the boys to tell them we were headed out and they were to take care of Nanny then joined me at the front door. Raising her eyebrows she silently asked why we were waiting.

I took a long breath and tried to dismiss the way she looked in those jeans. Really, she had that girl next door look down cold. When we stepped outside, she showed me three gold chains and two rings. "Nanny's jewelry. She said we can trade it. She said I can have her wedding ring, later."

My gut tightened, but it might be the best we could do. I told her to keep it in her pockets and not bring it out unless I told her.

The storm had left light damage in its wake. Shingles torn from roofs. Tree limbs down. A wooden fence was knocked over. But nothing devastating. Every window was dark. People were either asleep or without candles.

The morning sky was overcast and threatening to rain again. An hour before sunrise. The air tasted wet with a hint of moldy dirt, unusual for the desert.

Meagan's house was on a cul-de-sac, they were about halfway up. Without a word, I started down the suburban road then turned east towards downtown. As we walked, I kept a lookout for trouble, but it really was early. The storm had driven everyone inside. We'd have freedom for a bit. Or at least I hoped so.

"What are we looking for?" Meagan asked as she skipped to keep up.

"Food, weapons," I said as I forced myself to slow down.

"There's a supermarket two blocks over."

I shrugged and then started in the direction she had indicated. How many people are in Reno? I wondered. What, three hundred thousand with the tourists? That's almost a million meals per day.

I shuddered thinking about all these people trapped in this city and what it was going to get like when the food ran out.

The roads were clogged with dead cars, the occasional pile-up, but mostly just dead empty vehicles sitting in the middle of the road like lonely cows eating their cud. I made sure not to walk too fast and glanced over at

Meagan to see how she was doing. She caught me staring and blushed.

Okay, new favorite pastime, I thought. There was nothing so cute as Meagan blushing. We walked in an awkward silence, neither knowing what to say. The awkwardness ended abruptly when we got to the supermarket and found it blocked with a dozen men holding rifles.

They'd pushed cars in front of all the glass doors and stood behind the barriers denying entry.

"Are you guys open?" I asked, knowing it was a ridiculous question.

The large, pot-bellied man with the rifle resting on his hip shook his head. "No, we ain't opening. Go try somewhere else. This is ours."

Meagan gasped, "You can't do that."

He snickered and then looked at me as if to ask was she real. "Ain't no one stopping us."

"What about the police?" she demanded.

He laughed again then pointed to two police officers in uniform behind the vehicles guarding the far entrance.

"Come on," I said as I gently touched her shoulder to guide her away. It was obvious we weren't getting in here and we needed to stop wasting our time.

"No," she said as she pulled away from me and approached the man. "This isn't right, You're mother would be ashamed of you."

He stared at her for a moment then barked out a loud laugh. "My mother won't be upset because her grandkids will be eating tonight. And next week."

"Come on," I said as I tried getting her away before this turned ugly. She really needed to learn which battles to pick.

"That's right," the man said lowering his rifle, "You need to get her out of here."

"NO!," Meagan demanded. "I want to speak to whoever is in charge."

"Jesus, girl," I yelled as I wrapped my arms around her and picked her up to carry her away. "Will you shut up before you get me killed?"

She fought to get out of my grip, but I just held on and got her to the other side of the parking lot before I set her down. "Are you going to listen to me?" I asked before I let her go.

She gritted her teeth but finally nodded. Sighing heavily, I put her down then stepped back, ready to block her if she tried to go back there.

"This isn't right," she growled.

"There is no right or wrong anymore. Or if there is, it's changed. Don't forget, they have guns. I don't. I would prefer not to upset the people who can kill us."

She glared at me and then back at the store. "What are we going to do?"

I was tempted to tell her we were going to walk to Idaho, but I bit my tongue and shrugged. "We'll find something." One of my more stupid statements. We spent the next four hours walking through town. I swear, every shop or restaurant was either boarded up, guarded by men with guns, or already picked clean.

We were walking down by the casinos. Meagan pointed, "I was looking forward to going in there when I turned twenty-one. I wanted to see what all the fuss was about. But now ..."

"Slot machines don't work without electricity."

"Nothing works without electricity," she said with a sadness in her voice that tugged at my heart. We were passing a parking garage when I noticed a man pushing a flat cart piled high with boxes. The kind of boxes filled with meat for restaurants.

"Hey, where'd you get that."

He immediately reached behind his back and pulled a gun. I held up my hands and backed away. I think he saw we were no threat as his shoulders relaxed. "I work as a dishwasher. I got the last of it. There's nothing left. We cleaned out the restaurant. It would have spoiled anyway."

I sighed as I nodded. I could feel Meagan sagging with disappointment.

The guy kept the gun generally pointed in our direction as he pushed the cart up the street. I wonder if he made it home or was, he jumped by a dozen people?

"What now?"

"We keep looking," I told her, we really didn't have a choice. Three blocks later I noticed several people up on I-80. It took me a moment to realize they were gathered around the back of a semi-truck.

"Come on," I yelled to Meagan as I began to run. We had to get there before everything was gone. People, mostly men, were scurrying around the truck like ants at a picnic, ducking up into the truck, grabbing boxes then hurrying away before anyone could stop them.

"Stay here," I told Meagan as I parked her at the corner of the back of the truck. It was already two-thirds empty. Obviously, it had been enroute to a grocery store and was loaded with pallets of food. People were pushing to get at it.

I shot Meagan a look to let her know I was deadly serious then pulled myself up into the truck. I wove between a dozen men and grabbed the first case of food I could get at. I was so afraid of someone opening up with a gun to scare everyone away.

When I got to the edge, I dropped the case next to Meagan then ran back to get another.

"Chase," she yelled. I turned to find her fighting with an old man who was trying to grab the case of cans away from her. My heart jumped but I took time to grab two more plastic-wrapped packages then hurried back to her. She'd placed herself between him and our food, fighting him off.

"Hey," I growled as I dropped down next to her. I really didn't have time for this, so I pushed him down then grabbed our three cases of food and headed for home, the whole time expecting a bullet to the back of the head.

"I can take some of that," Meagan said, indicating the stuff in my arms. I noticed she didn't mention the old man I'd knocked to the ground.

"I've got a better idea," I said as I moved us to behind a car parked on the shoulder. When I was sure we weren't visible I started opening the boxes and stuffing the cans into my backpack. Twenty-four cans of chili, Twelve 16-ounce cans of tomato paste, and twelve cans of green beans.

When I had the pack loaded, I swung it up onto my shoulders and bent under the weight.

Once we were on the road Meagan shook her head, "That man, he was going to take our food."

I almost smiled. When did it become our food? We had stolen it. "You did good, holding him off. Thanks."

She blushed then asked, "How long will it last?"

I didn't have the heart to tell her less than a week, instead, I just shrugged and said, "We'll go out each day. Build up a safety net."

She nodded but I could see the worry in her eyes. I think the reality of this new world was beginning to sink in. She'd been in a fight with an old man over food. That wouldn't have happened the week before.

I would have missed the off-ramp that led to her house, but Meagan pointed it out and we headed down. When we got to her street I slid to a quick stop. Someone had pushed four cars across the entrance to the street.

A big guy with a pistol in a leather holster hung off his belt. About forty, he stood behind the cars looking at us like we were bed bugs wanting to get into his house.

"Mr. Gunderson," Meagan said with a cheerful tone.

"Meagan," the man said, never taking his eyes off me. "Whose this?"

She didn't miss a beat, "This is Chase Conrad. He's living with us."

"That's not smart," he said. "I don't know if we can allow that."

Meagan glared at the man and actually put her hands on her hips. "Are you going to tell my grandmother who she can invite to stay with us? Really? You're a braver person than me."

The man actually gulped then said, "We need to protect the neighborhood. There's already been people snooping around."

I wanted to point out that all a person needed to do was hop a fence and they'd be on the street. But I kept my mouth shut. The man still glared at me, moving to stand between two cars, blocking our way.

"I need to see what's in the pack."

"No," I said and moved to go around the back of the car.

"Stop," he yelled as his hand dropped to his gun.

I froze then slowly turned to him. "Are you going to kill me because I won't let you look in my pack?"

"Are you going to die to keep it secret?"

"Mr. Gunderson," Meagan gasped.

A tenseness hung in the air, each of us waiting, me waiting for him to shoot me. Him waiting for me to do what he'd told me. But what he didn't know was we would be waiting until hell froze over before I complied. I am just naturally stubborn.

Meagan's head whipped back and forth until she stepped between us and said, "It's just cans of green beans." Reaching into the pack she pulled out a can and showed him. "We got them off a truck up by exit 86."

I wanted to snatch the can back. How dare she do what the man wanted. But I held back and just glared at him, letting him know I was ready to die if necessary. I know, not very smart, and I'll admit I learned that staying alive was more important. I had people I was becoming responsible for. But then, at that moment, I just didn't care.

Finally, his shoulders slumped, and he nodded for us to go on. We'd just worked our way past the cars when he called out. "We're going to need guards. I'll mark you down for tonight, six to midnight."

Turning back I asked, "Is that a demand or a request."

Before he answered, Meagan jumped in and said, "A request," then she started pushing me towards her house, whispering, "Just go home. You don't need to piss off the entire world."

I shot her a quick smile and let her tug me towards her house. She caught me looking at her hand holding mine and blushed. Yes, there were worse things in this world than Meagan Foster blushing.

Chapter Eight

<u>Meagan</u>

Nanny was getting worse. One week since the asteroid and she was so much worse. Her ankles were swollen like melons, and she had a cough that racked her body. But it was the listlessness that worried me the most. My grandmother had always been full of life. Now, it was slowly leaking away.

Wiping at a tear I gave her one last look then gently closed her door. Chase glanced up with concern in his eyes. He had just returned from his daily exploration and came back with six empty milk jugs. As I watched, he filled them before adding a teaspoon of Clorox.

"If we ever run out of this stuff, we'll have to boil everything."

I could only grimace.

"How's your grandmother?" he asked. I was tempted to snap at him. Was he hoping she would hurry up and die so he could take off for Idaho? I still didn't plan on us going with him. It was too far, and this was my home.

Sitting down at the breakfast bar, I put my head down trying to push the worry out of my mind. The house smelled musty. Chase had explained that houses nowadays weren't designed to exist without air conditioning.

He'd insisted we open every window and the sliding glass door to create a cross breeze.

I was pretty sure it was useless, but I wasn't going to fight him on it.

He'd just finished the last jug when a shot rang out next door. I jumped and looked at Chase, but he was already rushing into the backyard. He jumped up on the air conditioning unit to look over the fence.

"Crap," he muttered under his breath as he shook his head. "Stay here," he told me.

As usual, I ignored him. I wish I hadn't. We found old Mr. Anderson with half his head splattered over the sliding glass door. Shaina, his black and white border collie was licking his hand, begging him to not be dead.

Shaina looked at us, pleading for us to make it all right. I took her collar and pulled her away, being careful not to step in the blood.

Chase squatted down and carefully removed the pistol from Mr. Anderson's hand. "I guess he didn't want to face what was happening." He then pointed to the spilled bag of dog food and said, "He left enough for his dog."

"Nanny told me a couple of months ago that he had cancer. He probably couldn't get to his treatments. And even if he could, would they have what he needed?"

"I don't know," Chase said as he looked around the room and then opened the door to the garage.

"What are you looking for?"

"A shovel. I figure we'll bury him in trade for all his food and this gun."

The coldness in his voice shocked me. Granted, he hadn't known the man, but you'd think he'd feel something, anything. But no, colder than frozen iron.

He did something to the pistol, sliding something back and taking a bullet out and then the magazine. He stuffed it into the waist of his jeans then grabbed a shovel and started for the back yard. I held Shaina as he began digging the grave.

I'll admit, there is something about watching a strongly built boy do manual labor. The way his body moved, like a well-oiled machine, every muscle working smoothly. He was a half hour into it when he stopped and wiped his brow before pulling his shirt off then attacking the hole again.

I returned to our house and got one of the jugs of purified water and an empty cup. He just smiled at me and drank directly from the containers, resting it on his arm like a stone jug full of bootleg whiskey.

He was stretching when both Austin and Jimmy stepped past me to relieve him. I hadn't seen them come into the yard. Chase nodded and handed over the shovel. While they continued to dig, he went back into the house and we wrapped Mr. Anderson in a comforter off the bed.

"That's deep enough," He told the boys. I was about to correct him, it was only three feet deep, not six. But I realized I wasn't willing to start digging so I better shut up. The body made a weird thunk noise when we lowered it into the hole.

Jimmy looked up. "Do we say anything before or after we cover him?" A shudder ran down my spine. My brother sounded just as cold as Chase.

"After," Chase said as he started to cover the body, each shovel full of dirt making a swish sound when the dirt hit the comforter.

When he was done, we stepped back, Chase put on his shirt then nodded to me. As if I was supposed to say something. Taking a deep breath I said, "Mr. Anderson was a nice man. And his dog loved him."

Shaina sniffed at the grave then looked back at us trying to understand.

Chase bowed his head for a minute then said, "Austin, find trash bags for the dog food."

"We get to keep her?" Austin asked in disbelief.

Chase nodded. "Next to a gun, a dog is the best thing to have. Always get yourself a dog if you can."

Austin buried his head in the dog's neck ruff.

"James, Get my pack." Chase then turned to me and said. "I want every bit of food, candle, tool, or weapon we can find."

I was loading up his pack when he whooped from the master bedroom. He stepped out with a smile a mile wide holding a box of bullets. I had absolutely no idea what kind of gun it was, but I was surprised to discover that I wasn't upset about it coming into our house.

Chase let out a long breath. "Now I won't feel so naked on guard duty."

We ended up finding two pocket knives that Chase insisted on giving to each of the boys.

"They'll cut themselves," I argued.

He shrugged, "Probably, but only once."

Rolling my eyes I was going to fight with him but realized neither of my brothers was going to part with their new weapon no matter what I said. I don't think even Nanny could have gotten them away from the boys.

But it was the food that was surprising. There were four cases of strawberry Ensure. Almost a hundred eight-ounce bottles. The cupboards had pasta and a five-pound bag of flour. But it was the medicine cabinet that made my heart jump. A large bottle of oxycontin pain relievers. These would help Nanny, I'd noticed her wincing every time I helped her to the bathroom and knew she was in constant pain. Pain more than Tylenol could handle.

We also found candles, and the most valuable item in this new world. A storm lantern with a bottle of oil under the sink.

After we'd moved everything back to our house, I added it to my inventory then looked at Chase with a big smile.

He shook his head. "Add a month, tops. This gets us to the end of July."

My heart fell. I'd felt like we'd hit a treasure trove. But he was right, five people ate a lot of food.

Chase turned to Austin and said, "Only one cup of dog food for Shaina. We've got to make it last. And no sharing your food. Understand?"

Austin nodded. Chase sighed, then left to head out looking for more food. That had become his life, either on guard duty at the cars or out looking for more food. I had stopped going with him because I hated coming home empty-handed. The look on the boys' faces was just too painful. Or worse,

Nanny asking how we did and having to tell her we'd ended up empty.

Later that evening, Chase returned holding up a dead rabbit. Gripping him by the ears. Not a scrawny jackrabbit, but a commercial, pet bunny-type rabbit.

"Where did you get that?" I demanded as I had to force my jaw to close.

He laughed, "I traded two bullets for it. A guy just off the highway had three of them. He wanted six bullets, I got him down to two. I guess he needed 9 Mil, and I was the only one willing to part with some.

"What are you going to do with it?" I asked, terrified he would expect me to skin it.

He chuckled. "Rabbit stew, I can stretch it out for two meals." He ended up cooking it all day. He cooked the entrails for Shaina then served us rabbit stew with carrots and the last of our potatoes and flour tortillas.

I swear a meal had never tasted so good. "You're a good cook," I told him as I took another bite. He laughed then shrugged.

I was almost happy and enjoying life when Nanny called from the back room. My heart jumped, the fear in her voice terrified me.

"Yes," I said as I rushed into her room. She held out her hand, begging me to come to her. "Are you okay?" I asked, knowing she'd lie to me and say she was fine. And she did look better than normal, with a little color in her cheeks.

"Chase," She said with a heavy sigh. "He's your only hope."

"Nanny," I admonished, "I'm not helpless."

She just stared at me. "If you were smart, you'd trap that boy. Bind him to you so tight he never gets away."

"Nanny," I gasped. How could she think like that?

"Don't Nanny me. Deep down, you know I'm right. It's just going to take you a while to finally admit it. The boy is tall, strong, brave, handsome, intelligent, and has a farm in Idaho. What isn't there to fall in love with."

"Nanny," I said for the third time then quickly glanced at the door to make sure he couldn't hear all this, I'd have died of embarrassment. Thankfully, I could hear him and the boys discussing arrowheads in the living room.

"I'm dying, honey," she said as she patted my hand.

"No ..."

"Meagan, it's true, and the quicker you accept it the better. It's okay. I'm ready. I'm only worried about leaving you three. But with Chase ... I can leave you with him and die peaceful."

My heart turned over as I tried to figure out what to say. Everything demanded I fight against her statement, but I also knew she needed to think we would be all right. She needed that reassurance to let go.

"Okay, Nanny, we'll go with him if we need to."

She sighed heavily then said, "Send him in here, I want to talk to him."

I balked then she smiled at me, "Don't worry, I'm not going tonight."

My heart broke as a tear rolled down my cheek. Grimacing, I nodded then went and told Chase that my grandmother wanted to talk to him. He blanched for a second then nodded. I watched him walk down the hall to her room and wondered what she would say to him.

God, please don't tell him that I liked him. No, I refused to force myself on the boy. He'd have to make the first move. It was bad enough we were relying on him for everything. I didn't need to add to his burdens, no matter what my crazy grandmother said.

Sighing, I closed my eyes and tried to see into the future. No matter where I looked, it didn't look good.

Chapter Nine

<u>Chase</u>

Stifling a yawn, I stepped into the house after my six-hour guard shift. Every third day from six to midnight I stood behind the cars and made sure we weren't murdered in our sleep. The street had come together in this one thing. Keeping strangers out.

In many ways, Meagan and the boys were lucky. The street they lived on was made up of middle-class strangers. Teachers, a fireman, and blackjack dealers at the casinos. The kind of people who didn't get involved in their neighbor's lives. No block parties. No drama.

I wondered when they'd start breaking. The second day after the last of their food I figured. What then?

When I stepped into the living room, I noticed Meagan curled up on the couch next to the storm lantern, a paperback on her lap.

"How'd it go?" she asked.

I smiled, this had become a thing. She always waited up until I came home. "Fine," I said, "Mrs. Cassidy thought she saw someone climbing over her fence. Turned out to be Miss Alverez's cat."

She smiled and was returning to her book when the night erupted with distant gunfire. Without thinking I pushed her down off the couch until I was sure the bullets weren't going to tear through the house.

It sounded like a full-fledged firefight, maybe two streets over.

"What is happening?" Meagan asked from the floor as she stared up at me with a strange look. Then pushed me away, "The boys."

"Sorry," I said as I helped her up. "It's farther away. We don't have to worry."

Her eyes were the size of small moons as she stared out into the dark. "Why are they shooting?"

Shrugging, I plopped down across from her. "Someone is trying to kill someone else. That someone is trying to stop them. As for why. Either food or sex would be my guess."

She cringed but I noticed she didn't correct me for being too negative. She'd learned the last couple of weeks that this new world wasn't all sunshine and roses. I joined her in staring into the night then took a deep breath before saying, "Listen, I have to go out for a little bit."

Freezing, she stared at me like I'd lost my mind. "Why?"

I scoffed, "Because burglary goes better at night."

Rolling her eyes she shook her head. "Just tell me what you are going to do now."

"I need to get camping gear, backpacks, stuff like that."

Her brow furrowed then she realized why. "I told you. We're not going with you."

"That's not what Nanny said the other night. She said you'd agreed to come."

Her jaw tightened as she glared at me. Wow, this girl hated being trapped. "We can't go all the way to Idaho, it's ridiculous, stupid, and idiotic all at the same time."

I held up my hands. "I'm not going to force you. But in case you change your mind, I want to make sure we have what we need."

"I'm coming with you," she said as she pushed up off the couch. "Let me wake Jimmy and tell him."

Grumbling under my breath, I cursed myself. I should have just gone and told her after. But I didn't want to spend the next half hour arguing with her, besides, I might need a lookout.

She pulled out a windbreaker for the cold night air then looked at me, waiting.

I led the way to the car-fence and pulled Steve Hamilton aside and told him we were going out and not to shoot us when we came back in a couple of hours. He didn't even question my sanity but simply shrugged and said, "No promises, but I'll try not to shoot either of you."

When we got out of earshot I told Meagan, "You stick close, be quiet, and do what I tell you. Agreed?"

She scowled at me but nodded. We spent the next half hour working our way through the streets. It was so weird, this total blackness, the occasional candlelight behind a curtain, and a gazillion stars covering us.

Twice dogs barked and once we saw three men scurrying away from us down a back alley like rats terrified of being discovered. Or cockroaches when the lights are turned on.

True to her word, Meagan was quiet the whole way. When we got to the strip mall, I held up a hand to stop here as I scrunched down to survey the area. Meagan kneeled next to me as I scanned the parking lot. Finally, I let out a long breath and hurried across the street, and dropped down behind a useless pick-up truck.

"There," I said pointing to a large sporting goods store.

She bit her lip. I gave the parking lot one last look then rushed hunched over to the front glass doors. Before she could stop me I used the but of my pistol to break the glass and reach in to unlock the door.

"Chase," Meagan gasped. "What about alarms? The Police?"

I simply raised my eyebrows. "There are no alarms. Not anymore. And the guards left two days ago. The company stopped paying them in food." Slipping into the store I turned on my flashlight and scanned the aisles until I found the camping section. "Here," I said as I held out a pack for her. "We'll need one for you and each of the boys. Plus a bunch of other stuff."

She followed me up and down the aisle as I stuffed first her pack then the boys' packs with camping gear. A spool of paracord, four water bladders, compasses, binoculars, fire flints, and three sleeping bags. A four-man tent, Fishing gear for handlines, two pots, and four plastic plates. Flashlights and batteries. Basically any camping stuff I could think of. It was like Christmas, just grabbing what we needed.

"Chase," she hissed then pointed to the front of the store. We both froze as a light swung back and forth. Without thinking I pulled my pistol from the back of my waist and pushed Meagan behind me.

"That's far enough," I yelled.

The light immediately swung, pinning me and Meagan as we ducked back into an aisle.

"Hey," a voice said from behind the light. "We can share, I just want some stuff."

I did a quick survey and knew we had what we needed. Shouldering the pack I helped Meagan into hers then yelled out. "We're going to move to the far side of the store. You can have this side. We'll leave you alone."

There was a long pause then he said, "Fair enough."

I guided Meagan to the other side then waited until the light moved to the camping section before hurrying to the door and out into the night. Meagan grabbed my free hand, her nails biting into my palm.

"What?" I asked.

"We were almost caught," she said breathlessly.

I didn't laugh, instead, I said, "But we weren't. So everything is okay."

She stared up at me and I swear I didn't know if she hated me or if she was going to kiss me. But something crashed in the store behind us pulling us both out of this weird world and back into the real one.

Holding her hand, I laughed as I pulled her towards home. She suddenly giggled and squeezed my hand. I could see it in her eyes. She'd never done anything wrong. A convict for a mother. Two younger brothers to care for. She couldn't take risks. But tonight she had almost been caught and it was thrilling for her.

Luckily, Steve didn't shoot us when I called out letting him know we were coming in. He saluted us with two fingers then pulled his coat tight as he leaned against a car.

When we got home, I was grabbing stuff out of the packs to place it on the counter when Meagan screamed from the back of the house. My blood ran cold as I raced back there. Meagan stood in the middle of her grandmother's room, her hands covering her mouth as she stared at her grandmother, dead, staring up at the ceiling with sightless eyes.

The room had that sour death smell that made me cringe. My heart sank. I liked that old woman, she'd had a hard life, but she loved her grandkids more than anything. I gently placed my hand on Meagan's shoulder. She turned into me and started to cry.

All I could do was wrap my arms around her and hold on for dear life as I let her get it all out.

Both of the boys heard us and came out of their room to find out what was going on. James froze when he saw his grandmother. Austin threw himself at his sister, forcing her to leave my arms so she could hug him.

"Come on," I said as I guided them back to the living room. Once I had all three of them sitting on the couch I said, "I'll take care of her."

"NO!" Meagan snapped and jumped up to storm back to her grandmother's body.

When I entered the room to help, she turned on me and ordered me out. "And keep the boys out until I am ready."

"Yes Ma'am," I said as I backed out.

The boys stared into the darkness, neither speaking. Shaina sat with her chin on Austin's leg, letting him know she was there if he needed her.

I closed my eyes and tried to map out what would happen and what we needed to do. It must have been an hour later that Meagan came out, her eyes were red and puffy, but she stiffened her back and said to her brothers. "Do you want to say goodbye?"

They looked at each other then both got up and walked to the back room. I held back. This was a family moment. Instead, I glanced outside and saw the first hint of morning. So I grabbed a shovel from the garage and started on the grave.

The sun had come up and was reminding me that we were in a desert when Meagan came out with a jug of water for me. "You missed breakfast."

I took a long drink of the cool water then shrugged before dropping back down into the grave.

"You're digging it deeper than Mr. Anderson's," she said with a frown.

"She deserved it," I said as I threw another load of dirt onto the pile."

She stood there in silence, hurting. Every part of my soul demanded that I fix it. Eliminate anything causing her pain. But there was nothing I could do. Nothing that would bring her grandmother back.

Finally, I had to stop digging when I hit rock. Five feet would have to be enough. Like Mr. Anderson, we lowered the body down then covered her with dirt. I stepped back and let them have their moment.

Finally, as we sat in silence in the living room, I took a deep breath then said, "She was a good woman. You should be proud to have her for a grandmother. She told me stories about her and her husband. She loved him. And she loved you three."

Meagan looked up at me with a scared stare, then she could hold it back no longer and pulled her brothers into deep hugs as she started to cry.

I sat alone, unable to help. But my mind was already focused on the road to Idaho.

Chapter Ten

Meagan

Two days of numbness. That was what Chase gave me. Two days being left alone to wallow in my misery. Both of my brothers went through the same thing. That lonely pain of losing someone and knowing you would never have them back.

Dad being killed had been a shock. A shock that took two years to get over. But this, this was different, a subtle pain, not as deep, but just as hurtful.

Like I said, two days was all we were allowed. On the morning of the third day, I came out to find Chase laying everything out on the floor where the dining room table used to be and on the kitchen counters. Four separate piles.

I knew instantly that my mourning period was over. An anger built inside of me, I wasn't ready for this. It was too early.

"Get the boys," he said. "I want them to pack their own bags, so they know where their things are."

"Chase," I said as I glared at him. "I told you. We're not going."

He stood up and frowned at me. "Think it through Meagan. Facts, not emotions. How long do we last? I mean, it's only been two weeks and things are already going bad. A

100

mob attacked the casinos downtown. When they didn't find anything, they started burning buildings."

Here he pointed out the back window, I looked and saw several pillars of smoke rising up into the morning sky.

"This town is filled with tourists with no food. No electricity, stuck in hotel rooms. Far from their families. Desperate. How long before they start pouring through the housing districts like locus stripping fields."

"We can't leave," I growled.

He sighed heavily then said, "We have enough food for two weeks. I figure it will take us four to six weeks to make it to Idaho. That means we've got to find food along the way. The longer we wait, the more food we've got to find."

"We can't leave," I repeated, but less sure of myself this time.

"Why?" he finally asked. "Why can't we try to save ourselves? We probably won't make it and will probably die along the way. But if we stay, we die for sure."

No, I didn't want to leave.

"Why?" he asked again, gentler this time.

My head dropped as I took a deep breath. "Because this is where my mom will come if she can."

His brow furrowed, "The mom who killed your dad?"

I gasped. I hadn't told him.

"James told me," he said. "Really, you're worried about her. James isn't. He doesn't ever want to see her again. I'm surprised you do."

A tear spilled out of my eye. He was right, but a part of me didn't want to face the truth. I just wanted everything to go back to the way it was before she shot my father. A family with problems, but a family.

Suddenly, he reached and took my hand in his, "Meagan," he said softly. "You need to think of the boys. They are your number one priority. If you want, you can leave a note for your mother. Tell her we're just north of Elmira Idaho."

Chase tilted his head then said, "We are going. Your grandmother made me wait for you. I could be halfway there by now. But I waited. I'm not waiting any longer.

I looked up at him, hoping, maybe, but I could see there was no way I was going to change his mind. He wasn't going to stay, and we would be left here all alone.

"He's right," James said from behind me. He'd come out of his room still in his PJs, rubbing his eyes. "You know he's right Meagan. We can't stay here thinking our mother is going to show up. And even if she

102

did, I wouldn't welcome her back. And you shouldn't either. Dad would be disappointed in us. Besides, she'd make things worse, if that is possible."

A sense of guilt at my betrayal ate at my stomach. My little brother was right. But Idaho? It was so far away. "Can't we wait," I said, trying to push this decision down the road.

"No," Chase said as he pushed past me to get his own pack and bring it out with the others.

I never officially said we would go, Chase just assumed so and started issuing orders. He had me and the boys pack each item. Explaining why we needed it. Food, Flour, the beef jerky we had made. Three pounds of rice, and a fresh jar of peanut butter he had refused to let us open. Water, tools, one change of clothes, two sets of socks, three zip-lock bags of dog food. All of it evenly divided. "This way," he said to the boys. "If we lose any one person, we don't lose everything."

Both of them turned white when he started talking about losing people, but he ignored them and kept packing his own bag. But I noticed that he took the extra stuff, tent, pots and pans, a small jar of chlorine, both the hatchet and the entrenching tool. The box of ammunition.

"Rule number five," he said as he came back from the bathroom. "Always pack more toilet paper than you think you'll need. Each of us gets two rolls to get you to Idaho."

When we were all done, he had me and the boys try on our packs and practice walking around the back yard. Adjusting straps, tying on our sleeping bags to hang from beneath the pack.

Part of me was still wondering how I could stop this, but another part knew we had to go. I made a point of gathering all of Nanny's jewelry, plus the things my mother left when she went to prison and my one gold chain. I stuffed them down a side pocket on my pack then showed it all to Chase. I put Nanny's wedding ring in a separate pocket.

He nodded his approval then folded his arms across his chest to observe the boys.

"When are we going?" Austin asked. "Tomorrow?"

"Tonight," Chase said as he grabbed the last two plastic milk jugs filled with water. We'd filled all four water bladders and treated them with the chlorine. One drop each. "This one for today," he said as he patted the last jug. "We'll finish two cans of chili and hit the road just after dark."

"Why at night?" Austin asked.

Chase sighed, "I'm hoping we can sneak out without being seen. Get away before anyone thinks to stop us."

"Why would they stop us," Austin asked, peppering Chase. I knew my little brother, he dealt with stress by obtaining all the information possible.

"Because, we have what they want. Food, ..." he paused then let out a long breath, "And your sister."

"CHASE," I gasped, angry that he'd said something like that to my little brother. Glaring at him I forcibly shook my head.

He scowled back at me then said, "He needs to know the truth. You all do. This isn't going to be a Sunday afternoon walk in the park."

A cold shiver raced down my spine as I saw the seriousness in his eyes. He was worried that men would try to take from us. Either our food or me. No, that was impossible. Surely our world hadn't become that bad. And not all men were interested only in young girls.

"I want a gun," Jimmy said.

Chase laughed, "I want a dozen more. But if we get one, you can have it."

"CHASE," I admonished, "You don't get to make those decisions."

"Yes, he does," Jimmy said. "He's in charge."

"Not when it comes to you and Austin."

Jimmy stretched his shoulders ready to argue when Chase put a hand on his shoulder. "Let's wait until we have the gun before we argue about who gets it."

My brother stared at me then finally backed down. Obviously deciding to postpone the argument. Instead, he and Austin practiced with their packs While I heated up the last of our oatmeal for breakfast.

That afternoon, Chase made us all take naps, then served up the chili.

My stomach clenched thinking about leaving. We were doing this, and I couldn't figure out a way to stop it. I swear, it was like Chase had become a force of nature. Both boys agreed with him. Of course they did. It was pure hero worship. The big strong boy would protect them, teach them the ways of men, and eventually guide them into the guild.

It was enough to make a girl grind her back teeth in frustration. My head told me it was the right thing, trying for Idaho. But I just hated it.

Looking out into the back yard I stared at Nanny's grave. Go, she would tell me. Trust Chase. It was our only hope.

We ate our meal in silence. Chase made us all go to the bathroom one last time. It was like we were going on a weekend road trip. We were walking across a desert, for crying out loud. I wanted to scream. He ignored me as he checked the packs, making adjustments.

I wiggled my shoulders and it hurt. Not bad, but it was annoying.

The four of us looked at each other in the dark. Shaina stared up at us, obviously wondering what we were doing. Austin had been placed in charge of holding her leash.

"Ready?" Chase asked.

"No," I said.

He laughed then opened the front door and left, expecting us to keep up. I growled under my breath as I herded the boys out and pulled the door shut, making sure it locked behind me. Suddenly I froze and patted the house key in my pocket. I would never be coming back here. Nanny's house. My home for the last two years.

Sadness filled me and grew even deeper when I noticed both of my brothers hurry after Chase. Neither of them showed the slightest emotion. It was like they were headed off to school. Just another day.

Adventure, I realized. Both boys were looking forward to having an adventure. Especially Jimmy.

A fear replaced the sadness as I realized there was every chance they would die on the road.

Chase waved to the guard at the car fence then told him we were leaving and he was welcome to anything in the house.

I hurried to catch up to Chase, "You shouldn't have done that. It's not your stuff to give away."

He frowned at me like I'd lost what little sense I ever had then said, "It stopped being yours the minute we abandoned it. You need to get your head on straight. Focus on what is in front of you. What can hurt you and the boys. You need to forget about the past. All of it. Surviving today is your only mission. Your only reason for living."

I studied him for a long moment. He was deadly serious. A fact that filled me with sadness. I didn't know if I wanted to live if the only thing was survival. There had to be more. So much more.

But, that was the thing about the road. There was no time to argue, discuss, ponder, or worry. It was one foot in front of the other.

The last of the evening light slowly left us turning the night black. Overcast clouds kept the starlight away. Austin was going to pull his flashlight when Chase stopped him and shook his head. Leaning down he whispered,

"Follow Shaina, she can see just fine. No light, no talking. Not until we get out of the city."

I gulped as I hurried to fall in behind Austin, putting my hand on his shoulder to let him know I was there.

Our eyesight adjusted enough so we could see about ten feet into the dark. Enough to avoid the cars stuck on I-80. I was fighting to keep my fear buried when Shaina suddenly started to pull at her leash, almost dragging Austin who fought to hold her back.

In a flash, Chase rushed past us to the front, his pistol drawn. It all happened so fast. Someone called from the dark, "Hold up, we just want to talk."

Chase ignored them pushing everyone forward as he stepped between us and the voice in the night.

None of us said anything as we scurried down the road, constantly looking over our shoulder, terrified whoever had called would come after us into the night.

Twice we almost ran into cars, both times Shaina guided us around them. Only after we'd run a couple hundred yards did Chase hiss at us to slow down. I had to bend at the waist to try and catch my breath. Running with a backpack needed to be an Olympic sport. I had never been so tired in my entire life.

Chase let us catch our breath then hurried us along through downtown and then out into the suburbs. We passed by a burnt-out motel with orange coals still glowing in the dark. Several times there were distant gun shots. And a dozen times we crossed paths with people trying to get into town.

No matter what, Chase kept us focused forward, always moving. Every hour he would stop, make us drop our packs for ten minutes, let us drink, stretch, run to the bushes if we needed to, then back on the road.

My back screamed, my feet felt like dead wood, and my head pounded. Have I mentioned how I hate to sweat? It is un-lady-like. Besides it just plain sucks. But even in the cool night air, I'd worked up a good sweat.

The eastern sky was starting to turn purple when I was about to beg that we stop. But before I could wimp out, Chase pointed to some trees lining the Truckee River. "That's far enough, we'll camp there."

Sighing, I forced myself to cover the last hundred yards then collapsed next to the river. Chase chuckled then said, "That was an easy night. It gets harder from here on out."

Ignoring him, I slipped out of my pack straps and rubbed my shoulders. Both of my brothers were doing the same. Ony Chase looked unaffected.

We three sat there and watched him set up the tent then hang the tarp between four threes.

"Two pieces of jerky each then grab some sleep. You can drink as much water as you want. We'll grab what we need from the river before we leave tonight."

"Tonight," Austin moaned. "How far to Idaho?"

Chase laughed, "About forty-five last nights."

Both Jimmy and Austin moaned. I closed my eyes and tried to pretend it was before. Back when we had cars and airplanes, and you know, things that worked to make our lives better.

Chapter Eleven

Chase

I lay under the tarp. Meagan and the boys were in the tent, but Shaina and I preferred the cool air down by the river. Reaching over, I ruffled the dog's neck and said, "Thanks. For last night. It's going to be rough. They're so ... innocent."

Shaina cocked her head as if wondering if I was disparaging a packmate. A sin in her world.

Laughing, I folded my hands behind my head and stared up at the blue tarp, and mapped out the trip in front of us. So many things could go wrong and decisions I made today might impact us a month from now.

And then there was the whole food issue. I mean, we were walking through the Nevada desert. Not exactly known for its wide selection or easy access to food. The recent rains had caused the desert to erupt with color, red, yellow, and blues. A gazillion flowers that would die out next week and none of them edible.

A serious doubt filled me as I worried about what I had taken on. Getting these three to Idaho. And what then? My grandfather would take them in. I wasn't worried about that. But then what?

And what about my cousins? My sister, all the way in New York. Would I ever see them again? Had I lost everyone? The permanent anger at the bottom of my soul started to flare up. Ever since I'd lost my Mom and Dad, I'd been angry at the world. And now this. It had ruined everything. What would the future be like?

Grumbling under my breath, I turned over and tried to get some sleep because it was going to be a long trip.

Later that afternoon I caught some trout and had them cooking when the others got up. Meagan shot me a quick smile when she saw the fish over the fire then sat down on a log and said, "Every muscle hurts."

I chuckled, "They'll feel better once you get moving."

She frowned at me. I knew she wanted me to tell her we'd take it easy tonight. But we just couldn't. I knew they were hurting, but starving to death would hurt more.

The night was a little less dark, an occasional break in the clouds let in faint starlight. We stuck to the highway. Again we passed people walking towards Reno. We were stopped for a water break when a group of three slowed down then crossed over the median to talk to us.

"Did you come out of Reno?" An older guy in a business suit without a tie asked.

"Yes,"

"What's it like."

I hesitated, If I told him the truth, he might ask to join us and I couldn't allow that. But if I lied it might end up getting them killed. "It's bad," I said. "Food's going to run out soon."

He scoffed as he pointed back behind him. "There isn't a lot of food in the desert."

A young woman and an older lady both in skirts frowned. They looked like they'd been put through the wringer ever since the world ended two weeks earlier. Scraggly hair, a ripped seam on a shoulder, scuffed shoes, and sunken eyes. The man saw me looking at the women and sighed.

"We were driving back from a meeting in Salt Lake, Our company is in Sacramento." He sighed again. "We got lucky. A Mormon family took us in. But a couple days ago they told us we had to move on." He paused for a long moment then sighed. "I don't imagine Sacramento is any better than Reno."

Meagan took my hand, squeezing it, silently asking me to fix their problem. All I could do was give them some advice. "If I was you. I'd head up into the mountains, close to the river where you can get fish and game coming down to drink."

The man frowned at me like I was the biggest idiot in the world, and I saw it so plainly, the man didn't know how to live off the land. It was as if I'd just told him to fly to the moon to solve all his problems. It wasn't going to happen.

Glancing at the women I looked at the younger one and raised an eyebrow, silently telling her she was going to have to find someone better. Someone who could protect and provide. She shot me a look, silently asking if I was up for company.

Surprisingly, Meagan saw it also and pulled at my hand. "We need to be going."

I gawked at her, she was never in a hurry to hit the road, but I saw the look she shot the woman and smiled to myself.

"Good Luck," I told the group as I slung my pack up onto my back. We left them there and I'll be honest, I didn't worry about them one second. Millions of people were going through worse. Everyone would have their own story. Those who survived would tell their children. Those that didn't, wouldn't.

I stopped everyone about an hour before dawn and moved them under a bridge over the Truckee River. "We'll camp here." There was no need for the tent or tarp, the bridge gave us shade for the day, and we didn't have to worry about cars or trucks racing overhead.

After a quick dinner of tortillas and canned stew, I made everyone fill up on water from the river, being sure to treat it with chlorine. "This is the last of the water for the next forty miles," I told them.

Both Austin and James gawked at me. "No water?"

"Not until we hit the Humbolt River. This was the hardest part for the pioneers."

"But," Meagan interjected. "There are gas stations, small towns."

"All on wells," I told her, "Deep ones. No electricity, no water. Besides, if they do have any, they'll be hoarding it. We can't count on getting any for the next two days. It will be what we carry."

I think Meagan wanted to go back, nobody had mentioned hiking through the desert without water. But she didn't. I've got to give her that. She didn't complain. She might have wanted to, but she didn't.

"Austin," I said. "Don't you give Shaina any of your water? I've got an extra canteen for her. You'll need every bit of what's in your water bag."

"Will it be enough?" Meagan asked.

I took a deep breath then nodded. "It should be if we don't get held up. We need to do twenty miles tonight."

"But all that rain? It rained two days ago."

"Except for some rock tanks, it doesn't hang around for long. And we don't have the time to be searching for pockets of water."

They seemed to accept it all and we were soon on the road. I made sure to keep them moving. Our hourly breaks were kept to ten minutes. One small sip of water every hour.

Maybe ten miles into the night's walk, the moon broke through the clouds flooding the desert in silver light. Meagan was leading the way when Shaina suddenly barked and tugged at Austin, pulling free of him, barking and growling as she raced past Meagan and into the sage bushes along the side of the road.

"Get her," I yelled as I dove for her leash, pulling her back as she growled and barked, focused on the bushes like a demon was getting ready to attack us, then I heard the deadly rattle underneath the sage bush.

"Freeze," I yelled at Meagan as I pulled Shaina back to Austin and told him to hold her. Only then did I pull out my flashlight and shine it on the bush. There curled up, ready to strike was a six-foot diamondback rattler.

"Don't move," I said to Meagan as I worked my way around her and shot the snake. The gunshot exploded in the night,

Meagan screamed, obviously surprised. I held the light on the snake and made sure it was dead.

Once I was satisfied, I cut off the head and tossed it out into the desert then started to stuff the snake in a side pocket of my pack.

"What are you doing?" Meagan barked at me.

I frowned at her, "Breakfast."

"Ewwe, you've got to be kidding me."

I shrugged. "Every little bit helps. Besides, it tastes like chicken. It's good." Reaching over I patted Shaina, "Good job," I told her, "You probably saved Meagan's life."

All three of them balked. Meagan swallowed hard then looked at the bush and then back at me. "I thought snakes didn't move at night."

"Not cold enough to stop them," I said. "They also like roads because the asphalt retains the heat."

All three of them moved to the center line of the highway.

I kept them moving, taking the lead. We were only halfway through the first night. A little later, Meagan scurried up to join me at the head of the line.

"Thank you," she said.

I frowned for a minute trying to figure out what she was talking about.

"The snake. If you hadn't yelled freeze, I would have stepped right next to it."

Smiling at her I patted her back. "You did exactly the right thing. You reacted the way you were supposed to. That is why you didn't get bitten. Some people would have freaked or kept walking while they asked why."

She seemed to stand a little taller as she let out a long breath. "But thanks anyway."

"Thank Shaina, I was oblivious."

We were silent for a moment then she said, "It is so scary here. I lived in Reno for two years and never visited the desert, just drove through."

I nodded. "Just remember, there are about forty-eight things that can kill you. At least the snakes warn you. Most of the other things don't."

Her brow furrowed as she glanced over at me, obviously she had wanted me to reassure her that there was no danger. Instead, I had scared her even worse. But she needed to learn. And learn fast.

We continued on in silence. I kept them going for an hour after sunrise but when I saw Austin stumble, fighting to keep his eyes open I found a small draw and led them up it.

I staked out the tarp across the draw and told them to settle down for the day.

I've got to give Meagan credit, she joined us in eating the snake. She winced and sniffed at it, but she finally took a bite then smiled. "You're right, it does taste like chicken. I thought that was just an old wive's tale."

That night, we were two hours into our trip when I noticed James sucking on an empty water bag.

"You went through it too fast," I told him as I shook my head.

"I thought ..." The boy looked devastated. He'd made a mistake and hated being thought less of.

"We can share," Meagan said as she pulled out her waterspout.

"No, we can't," I told her. "You and Austin are going to need every drop."

"But."

Shaking my head I said, "James can have some of mine. I figured this would happen, so I've been holding back. We'll make it."

She slumped with relief.

James scowled and fought to not cry. "That's okay. I don't need any. I can get there without anymore."

I didn't laugh. The boy didn't need me piling on. He already felt bad enough. Instead, I shook my head. "You will do what I tell you. Which means you will drink when I do. I don't have time or the energy to argue. Just do what you're told."

James swallowed hard, but he nodded. Good, he'd learned his lesson and really, it wasn't that big a deal. We had enough to get there. Or at least I thought so.

Chapter Twelve

<u>Meagan</u>

I ached all over. The night was endless. One foot in front of the other and we couldn't stop and rest. The whole no water thing changed everything. This was serious and there was no arguing. The facts were the facts.

It must have been two in the morning when Chase called for a halt. I watched as he splashed water from his canteen into a metal cup and put it down for Shaina. He then gave the water bag nipple to Jimmy. After my brother drank I watched as Chase stashed the hose back behind the bag.

He never took a drink I realized as my stomach clenched. How long had he been doing that? How long could he go without water? Yes, I know, it was night. Once again, he had been right, making us walk at night. I couldn't imagine doing this walk in the heat of the day with no water.

An hour later I heard that awful dry gurgle of an empty water bag from Austin. The look of fear and worry in his eyes tore at my heart.

"How much do you have left?" Chase asked me.

I shook my bag showing him I had a couple of swallows left at the bottom at best.

He took a long breath then let it out slowly. "No more breaks. We walk."

Both of the boys nodded, their faces getting that determined look like they were about to storm a castle.

We walked into the night. I made sure to stay in the middle of the road. We occasionally passed an abandoned car. Chase would always approach it first to make sure it was empty before moving us past.

And there were never any water bottles inside, I might add.

We didn't stop walking. I held out my hose for Austin. He shook his head, but I made him take the last of it.

Chase did the same for Jimmy then ran to the side of the road and found some gravel.

I frowned at him. He just smiled back and popped a stone into his mouth. "Helps with the thirst. Keep it under your tongue," he said as he passed out small round rocks to each of us. I simply shrugged and put one in my mouth.

He was right, I started producing saliva which eased my dry throat. But it couldn't last. We needed to find water.

We continued on. The sun was just below the distant horizon when Chase gave us the last of his water. "One last drink to get us there."

"How much further?" Austin asked. My heart broke. It had become light enough to see the haggard tiredness in his eyes. His skin looked blotchy and pale. A little boy shouldn't be put through all this, I thought as I fought to stop from screaming at any and everything.

Chase adjusted his pack and kept walking, "What's your favorite song?" he asked Austin.

The boy blanched and shook his head. "I don't know."

Chase nodded. "I've always liked White Christmas. Do you know the words?"

All three of us looked at him like he'd been taken over by aliens. I had to ask. "Why White Christmas."

He shrugged. "It was my Mom's favorite song. She'd sing it while making Christmas cookies."

My heart ached at the pain in his voice.

Jimmy scoffed, "Our mom never made Christmas cookies in her life. She wouldn't know how."

"Yes, she would," Austin countered. As always protecting his murdering mother.

"Boys," I admonished. We did not need to be airing our dirty laundry in front of Chase.

We continued on, one foot in front of the other. My throat burned and ached for water but there was none. The sun crested over the horizon bathing the desert in sharp yellow light. Highlighting the flat sandy terrain, the cactus and sage bushes reminded us there was no water.

We were fifteen minutes down the road when Chase suddenly began singing White Christmas. "I'm dreaming of a white Christmas. With every ...."

Our jaws dropped as we stared at Chase. He ignored us, neither embarrassed nor worried about being judged. His singing voice was better than average. But that didn't matter. He was determined to finish the song. When he completed the last line, he clapped Austin on the back and said, "Join me."

And that was how we spent the next half hour. Singing a stupid Christmas carol as we trudged through the Nevada desert. Only later would I come to realize that Chase had taken the boys' minds off their fears. For a short while he'd had them focus on something outside of themselves.

But even an old Christmas carol only holds a person's attention for so long.

Eventually, we fell into a silence, walking, always walking towards the rising sun.

Suddenly, Chase held out his hand stopping us then pointed down the road.

"What?" I asked.

"That green. Those trees. Do you see it? That's the Humbolt sink. Where the river plays out into the desert."

"Really," Jimmy said.

"The water is brackish, in a marsh. But a half mile up the river it's clear."

"How do you know all this stuff?" I asked him.

He laughed. "I didn't know any of it a month ago. But Your Nanny had a book on the pioneers and the settling of this part of the state."

I gawked at him. He'd just admitted he wasn't perfect which sort of made him even better than perfect if you know what I mean.

"Come on, we'll be there in an hour. We can go without water for another hour, can't we?"

We all nodded. He was right. We could do anything for an hour. Of course, it was not to be. We hadn't gone another hundred yards when distant gunshots broke the morning silence. All four of us froze.

"Sounds like two sets firing at each other doesn't it."

I shrugged, "How am I supposed to know? I don't have a lot of experience with infantry tactics."

He frowned then smiled. "The fact that you used the words infantry tactics correctly makes you way cooler than most girls."

I laughed, then the realization hit me. There was a firefight going on between us and the water.

Chase took a deep breath then said, "We go around. If we take a wide enough arch, we can hit the river way past those guns. Come on." And with that, he started south off the highway and into the desert.

"Chase," I hissed as I hurried to catch up. Then I remembered the snakes and the other forty-eight things that could kill me.

"Austin," Chase said, ignoring me. "Let Shaina off the leash. You guys stick close, and we'll be fine."

We had to work our way between cactuses and rocky outcroppings. Twice we had to help each other down into an arroyo then back up. I noticed Chase kept us perpendicular to the road and therefore the shooting.

The shooting was continuing. There would be occasional breaks then it would start up again. At least two or three guns on each side. I couldn't not wonder about what was so important that it was worth trying to kill someone for.

I came to realize the desert did not want us there. The ground was sharp sand with sharper rocks. Every plant was designed to hurt and kill. And the air was dryer than a dust storm.

"I'm thirsty," Austin whined as he suddenly stopped.

"What about barrel cactus," I asked Chase, "Can't you get water from them?" I think I saw it in an old movie.

Chase shrugged, "Sure, and that prickly pear over there, the one with the yellow flower. But they'll make you sicker than a dog. We're not that desperate, not yet." He grabbed Austin's pack off his back then nodded for him to keep walking.

My brother's eyes opened wide then he grabbed his pack back, slung it over his shoulders, and started walking.

Chase smiled then patted him on the shoulder as he moved past him to take point.

We continued on, dragging ourselves through the desert. Twice I was snared when I brushed up against a cactus. But we didn't stop. We couldn't stop.

Slowly I realized we had changed course, again back now more north. What is more, I realized the shooting had stopped. I glanced over at Chase. He just shrugged, "Someone won, someone didn't."

"Will they try to stop us from getting water?"

"There's a hundred miles of river. All the way to the Rockies. They can't guard the whole thing. We'll get to the water."

I wondered if he was just saying that to keep up our morale or if he really believed it. The latter I hoped. A confident Chase was so much easier to follow. Slowly, a long green line grew in front of us. The trees along the river, it had to be.

My heart jumped as I started to hurry. Water, I needed water. My body ached, my throat burned, and every cell in my body demanded water, now.

As we drew closer, I worried about the people who an hour earlier had been shooting at each other. Were they close? Would they try to deny us?

Chase suddenly held out his hand to stop us then pointed as he waved us down. A group of four men, all dressed in jeans and cowboy hats, were hiking up the highway on the other side of the river. Rifles on their shoulders and pistols on their hips.

We kneeled there in the dirt waiting for them to pass. All the while our bodies were screaming for water. Go, I wanted to yell at Chase. But he kept us back.

"Chase," I hissed, "They're gone,"

He glared at me and held his finger to his lips then slowly removed his pistol from his hip before nodding to the road. Two more men were coming up the road, one had an arm draped over the other's shoulders.

I swallowed a curse and waited. It was taking them forever to get past us. The wounded man dragged one leg. The other patiently helped him. What had happened? I wondered then immediately dismissed my curiosity. I didn't care. I just needed them to move so we could get to the river.

My knees hurt from kneeling, the back of my neck burned from the sun and my mouth felt like a steel furnace, hot and dry. I was growing to despise the desert.

Just as I was about to hiss at Chase again, he stood up and motioned for us to slowly follow. He continually scanned the area looking for threats both in front of us and behind us.

A long row of cottonwoods lined the banks of a small river. Really not much more than a creek bubbling over rocks. My soul soared when I saw all that clear cool water. I began to rush forward when Chase held out his hand to slow us down. "Not too much, not too fast."

I ignored him and dropped down next to the river and stuck my face into the water. It was like I became a sponge, soaking up every drop, replenishing a life force.

Jimmy slipped off his pack then rolled into the river. It was only six inches deep, but he lay back and let the water roll over him.

I turned and noticed that Chase had squatted next to the river, calmly scooping up water and taking a drink all while scanning up and down the river looking for threats. So strong, so handsome, so darn competent. Suddenly my heart melted.

We had made it. We had made it because of this man.

Chapter Thirteen

Chase

"We'll camp here," I told them as I began to pull what we needed from my pack. They were done in. I'd pushed them four hours too long. The highway was a hundred yards to the north, on the other side of the river, with a screen of trees.

After a breakfast of yesterday's tortillas and peanut butter, we all crashed hard, relying on Shaina to wake us if anyone showed up.

Again I slept under the tarp instead of the tent. I was deep into some dream about an airplane crashing and a pretty girl walking out of the smoke when something brushed my foot. I sprang up to find Meagan holding a finger to her lips, pointing upriver.

I instantly jumped up to find three men walking towards us, all armed. "Wake the boys," I whispered to her as I moved away from the tent to make sure they weren't in the line of fire.

"Afternoon," I said as I examined them. Three men, all in their twenties or early thirties. Jeans, long-sleeved shirts, and cowboy hats. I immediately thought of those men we saw that morning, the men coming from the shootout. I was positive these were the same men.

"You can't stay here," one of them said, stepping forward.

"We won't," I said. "We're going to Idaho."

He stared at me until Meagan stepped out of the tent followed by the two boys. Austin immediately took Shaina's collar.

All three men looked at Meagan like a man looked at a pretty girl. Appreciating what they saw.

Without thinking, my hand dropped closer to my pistol.

As if reading the anger bubbling just below the surface, Meagan stepped forward and smiled. "We will move on. Can we wait until dark? It is just so hot."

I swear, there is something about a pretty girl asking for a favor. A man just naturally wants to grant it. I could see it working in action. All three of these men stood a little taller, Two of them actually smiled. The girl had a superpower, no doubt. A moment ago there was going to be fighting and pain. Now ... now they smiled.

"Idaho?" the leader asked. "Why?"

"Grandfather's got a farm up there."

The man thought for a moment then sighed. "Stay out of the fields. We've got fields around the sink. Mostly Alfalfa, but there's other stuff. Stay on the main road. Until you're past Lovelock."

I nodded, "No problem."

The men examined us again and were turning to leave when Meagan asked, "Is there anywhere we can buy food? In Lovelock?"

Clenching my jaw I forced myself not to snap at her. They were going to leave, we'd gotten through the moment without anyone getting killed and she was dragging it out. We were going to have a serious talk about knowing when to shut up.

The man scowled and shook his head. "NO. No food." He then looked at me and said, "Stay on the highway."

I nodded then sighed when they left us. Turning to Meagan, I decided not to correct her on when to keep talking. Instead, I went back to the river and began filling bladders. We'd all drunk from the river directly, so I needed to keep an eye on them. There can be nasty parasites in untreated water.

"We need to find food," Meagan said as she came up behind me. "You said we only had two weeks."

I knew instantly that she was aware I was upset at her. "Yes, but asking those men was the wrong way to go about it. We didn't want to give them a reason to shoot us."

"They wouldn't do that," she said as she kneeled down to fill her bag.

I scoffed then said, "What do you think that shooting this morning was all about? Someone was trying to take food from someone else."

"How do you know that?"

"Because, those were the men we saw this morning. The ones who won. Besides, what else is worth killing for? Now? Today? In this world?"

Her face blanched but she quickly pulled herself together. "That doesn't change anything. We need more food. And I'm not going to eat snake every day."

I didn't laugh, instead I just nodded. "Let's get past Lovelock. Maybe in the next town, we can trade some of your jewelry."

That night we snuck through Lovelock without incident although twice Shaina pulled at her leash to investigate, and I knew we were being followed but she relaxed once we got to the far side of the town.

We continued into the desert. Occasionally we would pass a house in the distance with a storm lantern or candle burning. A dead gas station out in the middle of nowhere. Coyotes howled in the night. An owl swooped across the road on silent wings and the stars lit our way.

Meagan moved up to walk next to me. She glanced over at me but didn't say anything. Instead, we simply walked next to each other. Both of us scanned the road ready for danger. The dry night air had that desert coolness that you just knew would disappear in the morning.

"So," Meagan began, "Tell me your story. It's been three weeks, and I don't really know much about you. I know you know the desert, how to break into sporting goods stores, and all about camping. But that's it."

I nodded then took a deep breath and laid it all out. Why not? We had at least another month on the road. Besides, what else was there to talk about? I told her about losing my parents and aunt to a drunk driver. About my sister and me moving in with my uncle and two cousins. Just outside Tulsa Oklahoma.

"Why were you in the Sierras?" she asked.

I paused for a moment then said, "I was trying to get away from people."

Because of the starry night, I could see her frown at my blunt answer. "Instead, you end up being burdened with three strangers."

"You guys aren't a burden. Believe me, I've seen burdens. People who demand

136

special treatment. Demand to be taken care of. You guys pull your weight."

She shot me a quick smile. "But you still end up doing everything. Have you noticed? You build the fires, cook the meals, put up the tent. Tell us where to go. And, oh yeah, kill snakes."

I thought about it for a moment then said, "You're right. I need to start letting you guys do stuff. Something could happen to me. You lot need to know how to take care of yourself."

Her eyes widened at the mention of me not being around. "What do we do? I mean, where do we go if you're not here?"

I shrugged. Really, the thought hit me hard. If something happened to me, these three would probably end up dead. Or maybe Meagan could sell herself in the hopes of keeping her brothers alive. The thought sent a sick empty feeling to the bottom of my gut.

A few minutes later Meagan suddenly asked, "Why Chase? You have to admit it is an unusual name."

My stomach clenched. But really, I needed to just get it out there. "It is Chester, after my grandfather. My little sister couldn't say Chester. She called me Chaister, which became Chase."

"Chester Conrad," Meagan said with a smile.

137

Grumbling under my breath, I said, "That is the only time you are allowed to call me by that name. Never again."

She balked then smiled. "What are you going to do if I call you Chester."

I studied her for a moment then said, "Simple, I'll walk out into the desert and leave you guys all alone."

Her face blanched as she realized just how serious I was. I'll admit, it was harsh, but it was true. She swallowed then nodded, accepting the way things were going to be. "I guess that is why you call Jimmy, James because he asked you."

I laughed, she wasn't wrong.

We continued on in silence, a prickly silence filled with awkwardness, as I tried to think of something to ask. "So about your mother?"

Meagan winced like I'd poked her with a hot knife.

"Sorry, it's not that important," I said trying to ease my guilt. Maybe I'd been trying to get back at her over that whole Chester thing. Not chivalrous, I realized, both my dad and Uncle Frank would have been disappointed in me.

Meagan glanced back to make sure the boys were not close enough to hear, then said, "Our mother was ... Is, a narcissistic,

138

bipolar, depressive, with obsessive-compulsive disorder and I believe she has schizophrenia. That means she hears voices. Voices that aren't there. But the doctors disagree. Of course, they've never heard her mumbling to herself in the middle of the night. She's very good at hiding it.

My gut clenched. "Wow," was all I could say.

She glanced over at me then shrugged. "That is her problem. None of us are like her."

I could see the worry in her eyes. The fear that I thought they had inherited her insanity. "That must have been tough."

She scoffed, "Tough doesn't begin to describe it. I was always worried. My whole life revolved around Mom's moods. Was she up, or was she down? If she was down, was she dangerous, or just depressed? Knowing what to say and when to say it made all the difference.

"Your Dad?" I asked.

She smiled sadly. "He tried. Oh, how he tried. Always the buffer between us and her. When she was down, probably sixty, seventy percent of the time. He'd work all day, he was a mechanic, then come home and take care of us. Cooking, making sure our homework was done, getting us to bed. You know, parent stuff. All while she laid in her bed watching TV."

The bitterness in her voice was a little surprising. But I imagined there was a lifetime of hurt to justify the anger.

"But really, the up times were worse in some ways. She was like a maniac, doing a thousand things all at once and insisting we do them with her. Shopping sprees that lasted days. Once she decided she was going to paint our portrait. This from a woman who had never held a brush in her life.

"She bought everything she needed. Had us kids on the couch in our best clothes. She must have stared at us for thirty minutes. I could see it happening. The high of the up falling off a cliff as she failed to achieve her grandiose dream. The downs were so much worse when the ups crashed like that."

"I'm sorry," I said shaking my head. What else could I say?

Meagan scoffed then took a deep breath before she said. "Jimmy was home from school with the flu. Dad came home. We don't know why. They started yelling. Dad would do that sometimes. Especially when he thought us kids wouldn't hear him. He must have forgotten about Jimmy being home.

"Suddenly, she just shot him. Dad had a gun up in the back of their closet."

There was a long pause. "She's never said why. Not really why. But I think it was because he wouldn't agree with her delusions."

I nodded. What else could I do? "Like I said, I am so sorry."

She shrugged her pretty shoulders then said, "I imagine there are going to be a lot of orphans coming out of this. Our stories will pale in comparison."

I thought for a moment then glanced back at the boys. It was easy to imagine in that household that Meagan had been responsible for the boys. "You've done a good job. With your brothers."

She gasped, I don't think she'd ever been complimented about it. Looking down, she said quietly. "It is so much work. I am worried all the time. And now this. They have already suffered enough. They don't deserve this."

I was about to tell her to relax and let other people help when Shaina suddenly barked and tugged at her leash trying to get into the sage bushes alongside the highway. At first, I thought it was a snake and flashed my light only to discover a body.

Meagan choked, Austin squealed as all four of us stood there looking at a middle-aged man staring into the night sky with sightless eyes. Eyes the buzzards would take

in the morning. One more reminder that our
world had changed for the worse.

Chapter Fourteen

Meagan

I didn't squeal or scream. I guess I was getting used to dead bodies. All I could think of was that his family would never know what happened to him.

Chase shot me a look when I started walking again. I'm sure he thought I was going to demand we bury the man. But we couldn't bury everyone that we found. He was right, we needed to make sure that we survived the day. That was our mission.

The four of us fell into a silence as we walked. Occasionally I would glance over at Chase and wonder what he was thinking. About my mom. About our chances. About me.

Slowly the night gave way to a gray morning when Chase called the boys up forward and said, "James, you pick the campground."

James perked up, obviously pleased to be given responsibility. I knew Chase was implementing his plan to get us to start doing more things.

"You've got to try and find a balance," he told them. "Flat, with wood for a fire, close to the river, but not too close in case it rises."

"Why would it rise," James asked. "There hasn't been rain in days."

Chase pointed to the east. "It could rain a hundred miles away and flood through here two days later."

James nodded, "What else?"

Chase shrugged, "If you can locate the fire under a tree to disperse the smoke. And behind a bluff to hide the flames. A place that can be defended if necessary."

"We could walk for a week and not find all of those things in one place," my brother said.

Chase laughed. "Yep. Just do the best you can. But the longer you take, the more walking."

"What about me?" Austin asked.

"You're building the fire. And Meagan's cooking breakfast. Rice and beef jerky bouillon."

So our routine changed. We did everything. Chase would give us pointers and keep us on track, but we did it all, from putting up the tent to purifying the water. Within three days I realized we could survive without Chase. At least for a few days.

We timed our walks to pass through towns at night. Quietly, always dreading confrontation. Chase said we were making about twenty miles a night. I know he could have done much more but we were holding him back.

The highways followed the river. We had just passed through Winnemucca and camped between the river and a green field irrigated to grow alfalfa. Why it couldn't be potatoes or corn? I will never know.

The sun had just crested the eastern horizon. Chase looked off into the distance then said, "I'm going to that farm over there Do you have your grandmother's jewelry? Maybe I can trade."

"We should all go," I snapped.

He let out a long breath, obviously dreading the upcoming argument. "Meagan, Please. It's bad enough I've got to leave you guys here alone. But there is a reason we don't walk through the towns during the day. I don't want to draw attention to us. The same applies to farms."

My brow furrowed as I stared at him and realized that I didn't want to make his life more difficult. Besides, I was tired. "Here," I said as I handed him the three gold chains and the rings.

He sighed, nodded his thanks then told Shaina to stay with us before turning and walking into the desert towards a distant farmhouse.

Of course, I was too nervous to rest. What if he didn't come back? What if he got hurt, or killed? I would never know. I thought about that body next to the road and shivered. I could be like that man's family. Clueless. No closure.

Both of the boys were asleep within minutes, but I was just too restless and got up to look towards where Chase had walked. Please, I begged. Please be okay. I sat down under Chase's tarp, my back to a tree and watched.

Shaina sat next to me, resting her chin on my leg, looking up at me as if to say, 'I understand.' I swear, she had to be the smartest dog in the history of dogs. A deep worry ate at my gut. It wasn't just the thought of losing Chase. A thought that tore at my soul. But I knew deep down we'd never make it without him. Both of my brothers would end up dead. Starving to death in the middle of the desert.

Twice, the nervous energy got to me, and I had to get up and pace, always keeping an eye towards that farmhouse. So naturally, I missed him entirely. Shaina barked, her tail wagging a mile a minute as Chase stepped out from behind some trees. He'd come in from upriver, not in the direction I had expected.

His forehead crinkled as he frowned at me. "Why aren't you sleeping?"

I didn't roll my eyes at him. I wanted to, but I didn't. Then I saw the burlap bag he was carrying, and my heart jumped. "Did you get food?"

He smiled, "We got lucky, the farmer wanted to run me off, but his wife was nicer. That and she liked your gold chains.

"What did you get?" I said as my stomach gurgled with hope.

He smiled as he pulled out a cloth bag, "Ten pounds of corn meal. She said they make it themselves. Five pounds of summer sausage, and this treasure," he said as he held up a long rectangle wrapped in cheesecloth.

"Cheese?" I asked.

"Better," he said. "Lard. We'll get some trout and have a fish fry. We need the fat in our diet."

"Oh, Chase," I said as I moved to hug him then stopped myself. My cheeks flamed with embarrassment. Instead, I smiled and said, "I'm going to bed. Now that you're back safe."

He looked at me strangely then tapped his leg for Shaina to join him under the tarp.

Good to his word I woke to find four trout waiting for me to cook. And no, I wasn't going to complain about always having to cook. I loved dishing it out and making sure everyone got enough.

For the next three nights, we continued moving east, always along the river. There were fewer people. Either they had found shelter in the towns we passed, or there hadn't been that many out here in the middle of nowhere.

The sky had just turned gray, I was expecting Chase to tell the boys to find a place to camp when he suddenly stopped and stared at a billboard. I followed his gaze to see an advertisement for a town called Silver Creek, twenty miles off the road. Visit a working mine. That kind of place.

Chase stood in the middle of the road shaking his head.

"What?" I asked, suddenly worried until he smiled as he pointed to the sign.

"My great grandfather, on my grandmother's side. Guy by the name of Parker, he was the sheriff in that town. Cleaned it up."

"What?" I asked again.

"My grandmother told me about her grandfather. An officer in the Union Army, came to Silver Creek after the war, chasing his sweetheart. Ended up becoming sheriff, cleaned up the town then moved her to Oregon to a horse ranch. Two generations later, his granddaughter is backpacking through northern Idaho and meets a young man just back from Vietnam, a month later

149

they're married and she's a farmer's wife in Idaho."

"Wow," was all I could say.

He smiled. "I was just thinking. We're worse off than my Great-great Grandfather."

"What do you mean?"

"Think about it. The technology has been knocked back a hundred and fifty years. Back to just after the Civil War. But it's worse. Because we don't have the knowledge or tools they had back then. Does anyone know how to plow a field with a mule? And if they did, where are we going to find enough plows, enough harnesses, enough mules to feed three hundred million people?

"And that's not even thinking about fertilizer. And if somehow we could grow all that food. How do we get it distributed to people? Back then almost everyone grew their own food. You can't say that today."

My heart went out to him as he continued to stare up at the billboard. Finally, he shook his head and let out a long breath. And like that, the moment was over. We continued up the road until Austin picked out a camp spot.

As I lay down in the tent I thought about Chase's great grandfather. How cool to know that story. To know you came from good people. What would I tell my children? Turning over I forced myself not to cry and let

150

out a long breath. The story about my mom would never come up, I promised myself.

Three nights later we passed through Elko Nevada. Chase used his flashlight to confirm the turn-off to the northern highway. Suddenly I realized we would be leaving the river. "Are you sure about this?" I asked.

He shrugged. "We don't have much choice. This road goes through the mountains but we'll have water along the way, creeks, and some irrigation ditches. If we keep going east we have to pass through the salt flats before we get to Salt Lake City and then head north. This is easier. The road joins the river again about twenty miles up.

I sighed and nodded for the boys to follow Chase. The new road was a two-lane highway, a state road, not the interstate we'd gotten used to. What is more, this seemed to climb sharper. I could feel it in my calves in under an hour.

The sun came up, reminding us that we were supposed to be in bed when Chase suddenly stopped and stared off into the distance his jaw dropping. I followed his gaze and felt my insides squeeze shut. A black wall was coming straight for us.

It was bigger, thicker, and darker than any thunderstorm I had ever seen and reached up so high it was impossible to see the top.

"What is it?" Jimmy asked.

Chase shook his head, I could see him fighting to say what he actually thought. "I thought I heard something a couple hours ago but figured it was a thunderstorm up in the mountains." He continued to stare at the approaching cloud. "I was wrong. I think Shasta let go."

It took me a second to understand. "The volcano? How? Why?"

Suddenly he looked around and the color drained from his face as he realized we were surrounded by open flatness with nowhere to hide.

"Run," he yelled as he started to race back the way we had come.

My heart jumped to my throat as I pushed the boys to go. Suddenly I realized just how much danger we were in. The ash cloud would cover us. "Go, go," I encouraged as I fought to catch up to Chase.

At first, I thought he was abandoning us until I saw him slide to a stop and drop down into a dry creek bed. "In here," he said pointing to a corrugated culvert pipe running under the road. As we scrambled down he was tearing through his pack and pulling out the tarp. "Get in," he yelled.

I glanced over my shoulder and froze. The cloud had gotten so much closer. I could see it rolling over itself. Dark, menacing, racing towards us. We couldn't survive that, I just knew it.

"Get in," Chase repeated as he pushed me down into the culvert. Four feet high I had to drop to my knees. Both Jimmy and Austin had already scooted to the middle of the culvert with Shaina between them.

Suddenly the light dimmed as Chase dropped the tarp over the entrance. I could hear him throwing dirt onto the edges to weigh it down. I held my breath. "Hurry," I yelled. I knew that cloud was close and if he was caught out there in it he'd suffocate.

"Chase?" I yelled.

"Stay there," he said but from the opposite end of the culvert. Suddenly all of the light disappeared. At first, I thought the ash cloud was upon us but when I used my flashlight to see what he was doing I saw him fighting to tuck the tent in and anchoring it at the bottom.

"Will it be enough?" I yelled down the culvert.

He smiled then held up a hand to block my flashlight. "It has to be. We don't have a better option."

Crawling through the culvert he crossed over the boys then over me to get to the original blue tarp. "This is the side we have to worry about," he said as he tucked the tarp at the bottom trying to make it relatively airtight.

"What happened?" I asked as I tried to figure it all out.

"The asteroid. It had to be. It shoved the earth's crust all out of whack. It took a few weeks for the pressure to build up, but it finally popped at Shasta. About two hundred miles west of here. I guess it could have been one of the volcanoes north of us. But the way that cloud was coming in, I'd bet on Shasta."

"Two hundred miles away?" I asked. "That cloud seemed very big for so far away."

He shrugged, "Tells you the size of the explosion. Shasta's been plugged up for three thousand years. I wonder if the other volcanoes have popped?"

A cold fear settled in my bones as I thought about the seven volcanoes in the Cascades. If they all went we'd never make Idaho. "What do we do?" I asked.

He continued to look at the tarp then looked at me and said, "Pray."

Chapter Fifteen

Chase

A sick fear filled me as I held down the tarp. That cloud had looked thick and endless. I thought of the people in Pompei but reassured myself, they had been closer.

"Are we going to die?" Austin asked. His brother punched him in the ribs before I could reassure them.

"No, not today," I answered. I didn't totally believe it but I wasn't going to say otherwise.

Then the cloud hit. A soft swishing sound as the ash struck the tarp. No wind, just a deadly quiet like the greatest snowstorm in history. I'd overlapped the tarp two feet on either side of the culvert but still, the ash got in.

Meagan's flashlight showed it dancing in the white light. A fine gray talcum powder with a gritty feel. The four of us stared at it clueless as to what to expect.

"When will we know it is done?" Austin asked.

I shot him a quick smile. "Just plan on spending the day in here, maybe tonight also. I was thinking about skipping a walk anyway, give our bodies a chance to recover. This seems like a good time."

That became our day, hiding in the dark, hoping things wouldn't get worse. The culvert was about four feet in diameter with a thin layer of mud on the bottom. The metal ribs poked at my back. I grabbed an old T-shirt from my pack and cut scarves for each of us. I had them wet them before tying them around their nose and mouths. I figured we could trade off the water for less ash in our lungs.

Eventually, the boys fell asleep, their heads against the metal, each still wrapped in their jackets. I glanced over at Meagan and saw her fighting to hold her eyes open. Without thinking I wrapped my arm around her shoulder and whispered, "Get some rest."

She sort of sighed heavily then sank into me, resting her head on my shoulder, and was soon asleep.

I woke when I felt Meagan sliding out from beneath my arm. Her flashlight was still pointed up spreading light through the entire tunnel. She shot me an embarrassed look as her cheeks flashed red.

What? I wondered, but I was reminded just how cute she was when she blushed. Don't get me wrong. She was cute all the time. But blushing just increased it.

"I have to go outside," she said looking down at her hands in her lap.

"No, we have to stay inside," I assured her. "You will be fine. I know it's enclosed. I know you feel like you're going to get crushed. But you're not. I promise."

She stared at me for the longest moment, her cheeks getting redder, then said, "I have to go outside. There is a bush calling my name."

"Oh, Um, ... Sure," I said as I lifted the scarf up over my nose and pulled the tarp back. I was greeted by a gray day filled with dust and ash. But a person could live. "Go ahead," I said as I pulled the tarp back and scooted to get out of her way.

When she returned I took my turn. The sky was low with a grayness blocking most of the sunlight. Two to three inches of ash covered everything. Plants were gray. The ground was gray. A monotone world I thought. A moonscape.

I thought about the people close to the eruption. Imagine surviving the first three weeks of the end of the world only to get caught in a volcano's blast.

A thousand years from now, geologists would study the layer of ash, mark it as coming from Shasta then move on to study more important things. Would they ever understand why it had happened? Or the impact on the people who experience it. No, probably not.

Suddenly I realized there might not be scientists in this new world. We'd been knocked back to the dark ages. How long would it take us to crawl up out of them?

Then I felt the first raindrop.

Looking up I could only marvel. Obviously, a storm had come in from the southwest, the ash cloud from due west and they were going to come together directly over our heads. The storm was moving towards us, much like the ash cloud had earlier.

I turned to go back when the skies opened up.

Jumping into the tunnel, I shook my hair to get the water out of my eyes. Meagan stared back at me in shock.

"Wake up the boys," I told her.

"Why?" she asked. "Let them sleep. It's only a rainstorm."

Letting out a long breath I explained, "I don't want to be caught in here during a flash flood. Do you?"

Her face turned white as she swallowed hard then reached over and shook the boys. "We're going," she told them. "Before it floods."

I was repacking my backpack when I noticed a small trickle of water seeping in under the tarp. As I watched the small stream

159

grew, washing the ash out of its way. My stomach dropped. "Go, go," I yelled pointing the other end. Then started pushing them.

Suddenly the amount of water grew as the tarp edge collapsed. "Now, Dammit," I yelled as I grabbed the tarp with one hand, my pack with the other, and forced the others out of the tunnel.

A foot of water rushed past me trying desperately to knock me off my feet. My gut tightened as I thought about the others being swept away. Austin burst through the tent on the far end, then looked back over his shoulder to see what he was supposed to do.

"Get out of the creek bed," I yelled.

Shaina barked, and rushed past the boy and up out of the creek, showing them the way.

I grabbed the tent as I exited the culvert then scrambled up the side of the creek bed to stand next to the others. The rain pounded into us. All four of us stood on the edge slack-jawed as we watched the water grow in volume and speed. Shaina did the doggy shake but was drenched again in seconds.

What mere minutes earlier had been a dry creek bed was now a raging torrent. All I could think about was to wonder what would have happened if we'd been asleep. The rain had obviously hit up county long enough to start the flood.

From the corner of my eyes, I saw Austin shiver and realized we were standing in the rain. Shaking my head, I rushed back up to the road and found a guardrail. I draped the tarp over it and motioned for the others to climb inside.

"It will keep us dry enough," I yelled over the raging storm. The four of us sat under the tarp in the dark listening to the rain bouncing off the road. After we'd been under for a few minutes I heard Austin's teeth begin to chatter.

Meagan immediately told him and James to change into dry shirts. "You too," she said to me.

Laughing, I shook my head. "The last dry one I had I used for the scarves."

She glared at me for not having something dry to change into.

"What about you?" I asked. And no, I didn't leer. At least I don't think I did.

Her glaring intensified three notches then she harrumphed and grabbed the tent, wrapping it around her. Somehow she did that girl thing of changing without exposing anything then shot me a satisfied smile.

We settled down and let the storm pass through. Almost an hour later the patter of raindrops stopped. I stuck my head out of the tarp and saw the sky had returned to that gray, ashy overcast.

161

"Come on," I said. "Let's find a camping spot. Somewhere we can dry out and make some dinner."

I wrapped the tarp and tent up, stowed them away and we hit the road. It was strange walking in daylight. But we really didn't have a choice. Besides, we were in the middle of nowhere. The soaked ash acted like wet cement. Thankfully the road was mostly clear, but if you strayed off onto the shoulder you left permanent footprints that would be discovered ten thousand years from now.

We walked for almost two hours when I spotted a building up ahead. My alarm bells started ringing. A building meant people. People meant trouble. But as we drew closer I began to relax. A highway equipment shed. The kind of metal garage where they parked graders and pavers.

Smiling over at Meagan, I hurried to the large metal doors to find them locked. It only took me a minute to find a rock large enough to smash the lock and get the doors open.

"Chase," Meagan hissed, obviously upset that I was breaking and entering a government facility.

"What? Are you worried the government is going to throw us in jail? God, I'd love it if someone gave us shelter and provided us with food. Jail is a step up in this new world."

She continued to frown but that didn't stop her from following me into the building. Three large heavy equipment vehicles sat in the middle of a concrete floor. Just a large building for storing equipment. No offices, no restrooms. I had hoped for a minor miracle, but this would have to do.

"We'll stay here tonight and through tomorrow then hit the road tomorrow night. Give us a chance to rest up. We'll cook up a mess of cornbread. I'll see if I can get some fish. The river is only a mile away."

"Can I go with you?" James asked.

I studied him for a moment then said, "You can just go do the fishing. I don't have to go."

"Chase?" Meagan snapped. "He can't go off by himself."

Laughing I shook my head. "At his age, Ryan and I were camping in the back woods all by ourselves living off the land. Man, I wish I had my .22."

"This is different."

"Meagan," I said as I let out a long breath. "You are right, it is different. We need to revert back to when boys could take care of themselves. When we trusted them not to get themselves killed. James, you're not going to get killed are you?"

"I mean it," she said as she put her hands on her hips.

James stepped forward and said, "You can't stop me. I'm going fishing."

I had to smile as he ignored her and headed out the door. "Go with him," I said to Shaina.

Meagan stared after him, then at me, her brow furrowing.

"He's got to learn," I told her. "Especially in today's world. Besides he has Shaina."

"No," she said as she turned to follow him.

"You don't understand," I said as I gently held her arm. "Smothering him. Protecting him. It will hurt him more in the long run. He needs to learn to depend upon himself."

I could see the doubt in her eyes. It was easy to understand. Her entire life had been dedicated to protecting her two younger brothers from their mother.

"He's got to cut the apron string someday," I told her.

She continued to frown then turned and glared at Austin. "Don't you get any ideas? You're not old enough."

The boy stepped back, raising his hands as if to say, "What did I do."

She glared at him, then at me, then marched to the door and looked out to where her brother had disappeared into the desert.

I swear she didn't sit down or relax for two hours. The sun was just getting ready to set and I was thinking about going out and looking for James when Shaina's bark echoed through the tin building.

James followed her in, holding up a stringer of fish, crappie, large bluegills, and a three-pound catfish.

The self-satisfied smile he shot his sister said so much.

I leaned over and whispered, "Don't push it."

He nodded, but I knew that feeling. Taking the first steps towards independence. I knew it was my job to help him get there all while keeping him alive. Not an easy job in this new world.

Chapter Sixteen

<u>Meagan</u>

I was still seething about Jimmy defying me when we left the next night. Chase, Jimmy, it was as if they had hatched a conspiracy to piss me off to the maximum. The idea of Jimmy going off by himself into the desert. Remember the whole forty-eight things that can kill a person.

No. It wasn't right.

And yes, I understood the whole needing to grow up. Boys having to push their independence. But he was only eleven. And I wasn't ready for him to start breaking away.

Chase of course was oblivious to my anger. I swear, he was enjoying the silent treatment I was giving him. Again, one more thing to make me furious. I wasn't worth worrying about.

The lack of power in this entire situation was becoming unbearable.

We left at last light. The heavy ash cloud still hung over us blocking out the stars but it was no longer falling. The flat endless desert mixed the rain and ash into a concrete-type mush.

Chase said we could use one flashlight to make sure we stayed on the road. "There isn't anyone out here anyway," he added.

I scoffed. He wasn't wrong. We were in the middle of nowhere. Surrounded by flat desert and mountains in the distance. Nothing but cactus and sagebrush as far as a person could see. All of it covered in a gray ashy mud.

As we walked, I noticed Jimmy hurry up to walk next to Chase. Which of course made me grind my back teeth. So instead I hugged Austin. Big mistake, he pulled away from me and shot me a confused look. Like, yes, we might be in the middle of nowhere, but that still didn't mean he wanted to be hugged by his big sister. So uncool.

I let my head drop. My world was changing in too many ways too fast. I was losing the boys and there was nothing I could do about it. If I tried to hold on tighter they'd only rebel more. And Chase wasn't helping things. I mean he had hero stamped all over him. Big, strong, brave, competent in everything. Of course the boys wanted to emulate him. And at another time, I might have been okay with it. But not now. Not here in the middle of nowhere with the world ending around us.

No. I just wasn't ready for it.

The road continued to follow the river, winding back and forth. We stopped at midnight for a quick meal of cornbread and beef jerky then started again. The sun was getting ready to come up when Chase pointed to a sign. Wild Horse Camp Ground. He raised an eyebrow asking if we wanted to check it out.

When we got there I wished we'd passed it by. Six RVs were parked in camping spots and two partially collapsed tents in two other spots. The lake was just past the campgrounds. A cool blue inviting us.

Chase stopped and held out a hand to stop us as he glared at the campground. I followed his gaze and froze. Austin chocked. Half in, half out of an RV was the body of a woman, her dress ruffling in the wind. Her eyes were missing. Just black holes staring into nothing.

Pulling his pistol, Chase scanned the campground. That was when I noticed the bullet holes in the RVs. Each of them had at least a dozen holes. Windows had been shot out, and two of them had doors torn off their hinges.

"What happened?" I asked as my stomach clenched into a knot.

"I don't know," Chase said. "Food maybe. It looks like only a couple of days ago. Someone thought someone had food.

"But her eyes. Why did they do that."

He shook his head. "Birds."

"Come on," he said as he turned and tried to get us to move down the road. "We can't stop here. They might come back."

"Or still be here," Jimmy said as he pointed. We all turned to see a man looking out the window at us.

"Go," Chase yelled, pushing at us.

Suddenly a shot rang out and a puff of dust exploded a dozen feet in front of us. "GO, Go," Chase repeated as he stopped, swung around, and dropped to a knee as he took aim and fired.

I froze, gawking at him then another shot exploded from the RV reminding me we needed to be gone. Pushing at my brother's backs I got us to the other side of a line of trees then stopped and peeked around a tree trunk for Chase.

Two more shots erupted and my heart sank knowing he was out there with no cover. He glanced over his shoulder and saw that we had gotten away. He shot two more times, one right after the other. Then jumped up and raced towards us.

I held my breath, terrified I was about to watch Chase Conrad get killed. At that moment I realized if I had a gun I would have fired it to stop whoever was trying to kill Chase. One of those life-changing moments. Luckily, he slid around the trees and smiled at us. "Go, he might come after us."

We scurried back to the main road and then around to the far end of the lake. As we hurried I finally let out a long breath when I realized we weren't being followed.

"Why did he shoot at us?" I asked.

Chase shrugged. "Wanted what we had. Or was embarrassed that we'd discovered what he'd done. All those bullet holes were the same size. Done by the same gun. I bet he went through killing everyone, taking their food."

The lake was large and it took another five miles before we found a camp spot about half a mile from the damn that Chase thought was acceptable. I noticed it was down behind a bluff. The only way in was along the beach or over the water. No one could get to us without being seen.

"We'll crash here for the day."

"I need to do laundry," I said, "In fact, you all need to do laundry."

Chase nodded as he tossed the tent to the boys to set up then dumped his clothes out of his pack onto the ground. He kicked off his boots, pulled his belt, dropping his gun and holster and his belt knife, grabbed a bar of soap from his pack then scooped up his clothes and walked out into the lake.

"Chase," I yelled.

He ignored me and began taking off his clothes, the water at his waist. I could only stare at him as he scrubbed his shirts and jeans then himself. He dunked down rinsing off the soap then turned to me and said, "I'm coming out."

I couldn't stop from blushing as I quickly turned around. Finally when I got up the nerve I turned back to discover him wrapped in a towel hugging his waist. I will admit that I sort of gawked. The man had wide shoulders, a deep, muscular chest with a fine line of hair traveling down to disappear beneath the towel.

He gave me a strange look when he caught me staring.

Ignoring him, I tried to focus on washing my clothes next to the lake. I washed the boys' clothes as well, dreading the idea of facing Chase. He'd seen me checking him out. I wasn't willing to deal with the embarrassment so I pretended it never happened.

Jimmy strung some Para-cord between a rock atop the bluff and a log on the beach. I draped our clothes over the line and said, "They'll be dry before we leave tonight."

Later, when everyone was asleep, Shaina and I snuck a hundred yards down the beach and around a bend so I could take a proper bath. I had just rinsed my hair and was walking back onto the beach when Shaina suddenly started barking. That warning bark made my insides twist into knots.

Had the crazy guy from the RV campground found us? Was it some other danger? I swear, she hadn't been barking for ten seconds when Chase came racing around the bend, his pistol out, a look in his eyes like a grizzly bear facing off with his worst enemy.

"Are you alright," Chase asked as he glanced at me then quickly away.

I realized I was standing there fully naked and dropped into the water as I screamed.

Chase had the decency to look away, scanning the beach and out into the desert. Suddenly he grabbed Shaina's collar. Holding her back as she barked furiously.

"What is it?" I asked, the water up to my neck and my arms across my chest.

"Coyotes," he said, "A pack of them. You need to get back to the tent."

"But ..." I felt myself flush. The man had just seen me naked. No way was I getting up out of the water with him there.

As if reading my mind he stepped forward a dozen steps, pulling Shaina with him. "hurry up and get dressed. I won't look.""

"Promise?"

"I promise."

Still, I hesitated. "I swear if you ..."

He scoffed and shook his head while keeping focused towards where he'd seen the coyotes. "Meagan, have I ever broken a promise to you? Besides, we have bigger problems than me seeing you without your clothes on."

He was right, he had never even come close to being dishonest with me. No, I realized. One of Chase's many values was his honesty. And sense of honor.

Glaring at him I slowly walked up out of the lake and quickly dried off, all the while keeping focused on him.

Shaina looked over her shoulder at me then refocused on the coyotes off in the distance.

"Okay," I said as I wrapped my hair in the towel.

Chase shot me a quick smile then nodded for me to precede him back to the tent.

"Are they dangerous?" I asked.

He shrugged. "Not as much as wolves. But ... if they got hungry enough, in a pack, maybe they might attack a young boy. Or if one of them is rabid."

My heart almost stopped, obviously one of the forty-eight things in the desert that can kill you. Suddenly I remembered standing in the water and him glancing over at me. There had been a look in his eyes that I didn't fully understand. I wished desperately I could ask him. But this was one topic we were never going to discuss.

So of course he nudged my shoulder with his and said, "The next time you want to take a bath. Let me know and I'll guard you."

He raised his eyebrow and was obviously fighting to not grin from ear to ear. I slapped his arm and said, "Shut up, go away, and never talk to me again."

He laughed all the way back to the tent.

Chapter Seventeen

<u>Chase</u>

I used some Para cord to set some trot lines out. I had the boys catch some perch and used them for bait. I tied forty feet of paracord to a rock, set the hooks six feet apart then walked it out and tossed it another dozen feet.

When we woke up I pulled in a Two and a half pound catfish and smiled at the others. We'd have a nice meal before we began our evening hike. Shaina ate every bit of anything left over, including the head.

The lake was on a high plateau, we'd been climbing ever since Reno. Somewhere behind us, we'd crossed out of the Great Basin watershed and into the Columbia River watershed. Now we were headed down slightly as the lake spilled over into the Owyhee River and wove its way through some canyons.

I turned to the boys. "Back there, the water petered out in the middle of the desert at the Humbolt sink. Remember after crossing the forty-mile gap. This water will end up in the Pacific."

Both boys shrugged, not giving a rat's behind about where water was going to end up. They were focusing on putting one foot in front of the other.

I almost laughed. A month prior I'd been deep in the Sierras. And now I was hiking through a part of the country I never expected to see. Beautiful, but tough.

Glancing over at Meagan, I had to smile. Which immediately made me think about her walking out of the lake. I probably shouldn't be obsessing about it in my mind. But come on. The girl was beautiful. And like this land. Tough.

I had to force myself to think about other things. I did an inventory and shuddered. We were running low on everything. We had enough cornmeal for one pan of cornbread. Two cups of rice, and a few strips of jerky.

If it hadn't been for the fish along the way we never would have made it this far. Plus, we were burning calories. A lot of calories. And the boys were still growing. They needed protein. We all needed fat in our diet. Something to fuel all this walking.

My stomach tightened as I thought about how much we needed and how far away we were from any help.

Once they were settled the next morning, I patted my leg for Shaina to come with me then stepped out into the desert. As we'd left the plateau the terrain had slowly begun to change. The river banks were covered in green grass and cottonwoods. The occasional pine or cedar grew in the hills. The rest was still desert, sage, and cactus but more tuffs of brown grass. There were still patches of gray ash, but less than had hit us and the rain had washed most of it into gullies.

When I found what I was looking for I began setting snares. Six of them, marking them in my mind then returned to camp and crashed.

Later that afternoon, while Jimmy fished the river which was little more than a creek at this point, I ran my snares and smiled when I found a desert cottontail in the third snare. If we kept this up, between the fish and the rabbits we could last weeks.

My stomach boiled though. I knew it wouldn't last. We had been lucky. No people. But a person can't live on fish and rabbits for long. Not walking twenty miles a day.

I roasted the rabbit and served it with the last of our rice. I cooked up the entrails for Shaina then we hit the road.

About halfway through the night Meagan stopped and shined her flashlight onto a highway sign. Mountain City.

Glancing up the road I couldn't see anything but darkness. My stomach clenched up thinking about walking through some town. We'd been out in the middle of nowhere for so long that I'd gotten used to it. Preferred it, in fact.

No people meant no trouble. She looked at me, the light showing me her questioning brow. I let out a long breath then nodded as I told Austin to put Shaina on the leash and for Meagan to cut the light.

The night air smelled of sage and juniper with a cool chill. We had just reached the edge of the town, six broken-down houses, three trailers, and a dive bar along the side of the road. The place was little more than a ghost town. Suddenly a dog barked, there was a flash of light from someone striking a match. A heavy glow as they lit a storm lantern and opened the door.

"Who's there," An old man yelled as he held up the lamp with one hand while holding back a German Sheppard with the other.

A sudden fear filled me. If he let the dog go it'd tangle with Shaina. He might be armed. And we had a whole town to get through.

"It's me, Sir. Chase Caldwell. Just trying to get home before my Mom notices me gone."

I swear the words just bubbled out of me as I waved the others on, wanting distance incase this guy started shooting.

He frowned then yelled, "Get out of here. Let a man sleep why don't you."

"Yes sir," I yelled and hurried after the others.

Meagan shot me a strange look when I caught up with them. "You breaking curfew. I bet that happened more than once."

I laughed, at least she was talking to me again. The whole silent treatment because of Jimmy thing had been forgotten. At least until the next time.

We hurried through the town. Five miles later we entered the Duck Valley Indian Reservation. "Shoshone and Paiute," I said to James questioning eyebrows. "We'll crash for a couple of hours but then take off at noon. We need food and the town of Owyhee is about five miles further.

Meagan's brow furrowed as she silently questioned me. I shrugged. "We don't have a choice. We need to find food. We'll never make it unless we do."

She sighed heavily then nodded.

Later as we were packing up, Shaina suddenly barked and then turned to face the desert. I turned to find three men on horseback trotting towards us. I instinctively touched my gun on my hip to make sure it was still there.

Three men, all with long black hair, one of them in a long braid, pulled up to glare down at us. In cowboy hats and jeans, they looked like they'd grown up on horseback.

Native Americans, one with a rifle across his lap.

The older one stared at us, cataloging and evaluating. I couldn't help but think that living closer to the land, I would bet they hadn't been impacted too much by the asteroid. Their world had held together so much more than the supposedly modern society. Anyone out here would be better off away from the cities.

"You don't belong here," he said, not mean, just a statement of fact.

"We're just passing through," I told him as my stomach clenched. This could go so bad so quick.

He frowned then asked, "Where you going? Where you coming from?"

"Reno," I said. "We're headed to northern Idaho, my grandfather has a farm."

His frown deepened. "That is a long walk."

I nodded, "We don't have a choice."

He continued to frown as he studied the two young boys then Meagan. I needed his attention back on me. "Is there anywhere we can work for food?"

Ignoring me, he asked Meagan, "Are you sure you want to do this? Like I said, it is a long walk."

She smiled sweetly up at the man then said, "Like he said, we don't have a choice. The cities are crazy. The small towns won't let us in. The farmers are afraid. The only safety is with family."

The man thought for a long moment then turned to me. "Stop at the Food Distribution Center in town. They might have something. Tell them John White Tail sent you. It's for Indians and residents of the town. But they might have something for you. I don't think the Bureau is going to care."

A food distribution center? Wow, could we be so lucky? "Thank you."

He continued to frown then said, "Be off the Res by tomorrow. That includes the Idaho side."

My instincts were to push back. How dare he tell me where I could and could not go. But my dad didn't raise an idiot. Things had changed. This was their home. Of course, it had always been their home, but now they got to decide who could and could not stay.

"Yes sir," I said, nodding, letting him know that I understood the new reality.

As the road followed the stream I noticed green fields off to the left, mountains rising on the right.

"Alfalfa," I said shaking my head. "Irrigated."

"Doesn't anyone grow people food anymore," Meagan said.

"Feed for cattle," I said as I pointed to a distant heard munching a giant hay bale.

"Think of the steaks," James said with a longing tone.

I laughed, "Think of the bullet to the head, or the long drop on a short rope if you tried taking one of them. People around here don't put up with rustling their cattle."

The town of Owyhee straddled the road with a school, clinic, and a small motel. Houses and trailers laid out in no particular plan. Population of about a thousand. Just think, this was the largest settlement for literally hundreds of miles in any direction.

The Food distribution center was one block over. I held my breath as I knocked at the door.

"Maybe we should just go in," Austin said.

I shrugged then tried the door. It was locked. My heart fell. The place was closed up tighter than Fort Knox.

Stepping back I was looking for a sign about their hours thinking about what John White Tail had said. Be off the reservation by tomorrow. I knew he'd send people to make sure we were. We couldn't wait for this place to open. But we needed food.

I was looking around hoping to find someone to help when the door opened behind me. A heavy-set woman of about forty with long salt and pepper hair poked her head out and looked at us, frowning. "We're not open."

My heart fell. Meagan stepped forward and smiled at the woman. "Mr. John White Tail sent us. He said we might be able to get some food."

The woman's frown deepened.

"We've come all the way from Reno," Meagan said with the sweet tone of someone who wants to be your best friend. "And we're out of food. We'll work. Anything."

The woman looked us over then sighed heavily as she opened the door. "You don't qualify. But ... I guess the inspector won't be looking at the books. They say nothing works anymore."

I held my breath as I stepped into a room lit in yellow light from a storm lantern. The woman saw me staring at it and shook her head. "I don't know what we're going to do when we run out of lamp oil."

Thinking about the lamp and oil we'd left at Nanny's house I could only nod as I turned and examined the room. Shelves lined the walls with two aisles down the middle. Some of the shelves were bare. Others still had some items left.

"I don't think we'll be getting any more. Do you? I mean, is it really that bad?"

I sighed heavily then nodded. "Yes, it is. Cars, trucks, electricity, it's never coming back."

The woman didn't blanch, simply shook her head then waved for us to follow her.

"Here," she said as she pulled a ten-pound bag of flour and a three-pound bag of rice off the shelves and handed them to Meagan. Next a six-pack of large raisin boxes. She then looked over at the boys and sighed as she pulled four cans of tuna and four cans of pineapples off the shelves.

"I can't give you more. Like I said, we won't be restocked." She then quickly added two large cans of canned beef and two of Spam.

"This is wonderful," Meagan said giving the woman a beautiful smile. "Thank you so much. You don't know how much you have helped us."

The woman glanced down, obviously not wanting the thanks then pointed to the door for us to go. "And if anyone asks. You tell them John White Tail said it was okay. They'll leave you alone."

"Thank you," Austin said then smiled at the woman who smiled back for the first time since we met her. The boy was a natural charmer.

"Let's get through town," I told them as I stuffed my pack with the food. "We'll walk through the night until we are off on the other side of the reservation."

Meagan smiled at me, "Do you think we'll make it now? Is this enough? How much further."

My heart broke when I had to tell them we were only about halfway. And something told me the hard part was still in front of us.

Chapter Eighteen

Meagan

A full stomach and a mind at rest. Two of the most valuable things on this earth. More valuable than the largest diamond or a bank full of money. I was coming to realize what was truly important.

Health and a lack of fear about the future. With all this food, we could go for weeks. At least we could if we added fish and rabbits.

We didn't cross off the reservation until an hour after first light. When we crossed I turned to look back and saw three men on horseback in the distance watching us. I gave them a friendly wave then joined my brothers in searching for a place to camp.

We found a creek with enough water and just enough dried wood to cook up a meal of tortillas and fried spam with raisins for dessert. It was one of the best meals in my life.

That evening, Chase suggested we stay another day, "We have water and firewood, our bodies could use a day to recuperate. We've got the food."

I studied him for a moment wondering if there was some ulterior motive but no, he just thought we needed the rest. So we sat around the small fire. I swear within about an hour I was feeling twitchy. I needed to be up and doing. No one was talking. Each of us was lost in our own world.

Austin suddenly stood up and pushed at his lower back like an old man then smiled. "I think we should keep walking. I'm bored."

Chase laughed then looked at each of us. I nodded. I wanted to be moving.

So we ended up packing the tent and setting off into the night. The high ash cloud had moved through leaving us a sky filled with stars. I caught Chase staring up at them as he walked.

"What?" I asked.

He smiled sadly. "I wonder if we'll ever get back up there? Ever get off this planet again."

The sadness in his eyes reminded me that Chase was deeper than he let on. He wasn't just a big strong protector. Provider of sustenance. No, there were layers to Chase Conrad that most people would never see.

I thought about how he interacted with my brothers. Both a teacher and friend. How he was always putting himself between us and any danger. How he seemed to know what to do every time. Without hesitation. How did a person become so confident? I questioned myself a thousand times a day and never felt like I knew beyond a doubt that I'd done the right thing.

Chase didn't seem to eat himself up about things. Something I admired because I lacked the ability.

We had to walk two hours past sunrise because we were between creeks. The sun blazed across the desert and I knew it would be a scorcher later that afternoon. In the far distance, a black buzzard circled, waiting for its next meal. The desert was mixed with sparse grassland and endless sagebrush stretching to the horizon. With a gentle wind out of the west filling the air with a dusty savory aroma.

We could see a green belt about a mile in front when Jimmy suddenly yelled "Wow," and pointed. I turned to see a herd of wild horses racing across the desert. Wild mustangs, so beautiful. So free.

We stood and watched them dip down into a draw then back up the far side only to disappear into the horizon a few minutes later.

"I never thought I would see something like that," I said.

Chase shook his head. "They won't last."

"What? Why?" I gasped, almost as if my feelings had been hurt. How could he say that?

"Because," he answered calmly. "Before, we didn't need them. They were allowed to roam free, culled every so often to stop them from overgrazing a range. But free. Now, we will need their horsepower. Every one of them can be turned into a labor-saving device. Hundreds of thousands of people, no millions, have no way to get anywhere. No way to move goods, food. Believe me, someone will figure out to use the wild horses."

My heart fell as I realized he was right.

"Why can't people just leave them alone?" Austin asked. I knew his affinity with animals meant he would always take their side.

Chase smiled softly then said, "Humans have exploited nature. Tamed it. Shifted it to comply with our wishes."

"That's not right," Austin said. "It's not fair."

Chase studied him for a minute then said. "Okay, who dies? Do you want to be the one to pick which babies die in their mother's arms because their mother can't produce milk because she's starving to death? How about the kids your age? If we didn't shape nature to our wishes only one out of a hundred will live. Do you want to be the one who picks the other ninety-nine to die?"

Austin looked back, his mouth open as his mind fought to figure it all out.

Chase patted him on the shoulder. "What would you do to keep Meagan and James alive?"

"Anything," he whispered back.

"Exactly, and taming those horses might mean the difference for some man's daughter living or not."

"But there should be some way to do both."

Chase just shook his head. "You figure out a way you let me know." He then pointed to a spot down by a creek. Within minutes we had the tent set up, Chase's tarp, and a small fire going. We cooked up some rice and a can of beef then settled in but I couldn't sleep. Austin and Chase's talk still echoed in my mind.

Chase was right. I knew it intellectually but I just didn't want to face the consequences. Because what Chase hadn't said was. We had spent millennia shaping nature to our benefit. But now we couldn't. Not like we had. How did we survive, all eight billion of us if we couldn't shape nature to our needs?

We couldn't. Survive that is. Suddenly a hopelessness filled me as I began to wonder how many people would have to die before humanity was in alignment with this new state of being.

A sick empty feeling deep inside made me restless. I wormed my way out of the tent without waking the boys to find Chase up on one elbow, handsome as ever, his brow furrowed as he stared at me.

"I need to go for a walk," I hissed then started up the creek.

Chase laughed, "We just walked twenty miles. That wasn't enough for you?"

Ignoring him I worked my way around two bends in the creek, keeping an eye out for snakes, scorpions, and any of the other forty-eight things that could kill me. I was probably a hundred yards past our campsite when I stopped and sighed heavily. This wasn't helping.

I felt a restless energy fill me. I wanted to scream and I didn't even know why. I was still pacing back and forth next to the creek when I heard Chase gently call my name, "Meagan?"

Rolling my eyes I said, "I'm here. I'm okay." I knew by the tone of his voice that he was worried about me. A fact that sent a warmth through me. But also pissed me off. Don't ask me why.

When he came around the bend I couldn't help but admire the man. Wide shoulders, square jaw. And Intelligent eyes. He moved like a big cat. Floating through the land without leaving a mark. A man in tune with his environment.

My heart turned over as I realized I was falling in love with Chase Conrad. Okay, I'll be honest, I'd probably been in love with him the first time I saw him walk out of the forest. Tall and strong.

But now, I was finally willing to admit it.

Of course he would never know. I'm no idiot. No way was I adding that pressure to his burdens. The thought of being laughed at sent a cold shiver down my spine. Instead, I gave him my friend's smile. The one that said I was glad to see him. Not the one that said I wanted him desperately. You know the difference. It's all in the eyes.

He looked around then frowned at me. "I left Shaina with the boys."

Taking a deep breath I felt the antsy restlessness leave me. Now I understood what I was feeling and why. Now things made sense. "I'm okay. We can go back now."

Chase shot me a strange look then shrugged and led the way back to the camp but I didn't feel like going to sleep. Not yet, so instead I dipped down under the cover of the tarp and silently asked if it was okay.

He shrugged then joined me. Shaina nuzzled in next to me, laying her chin on my leg. I think she knew I was troubled.

"What's bothering you?" Chase asked. The boy really was amazing. So perfect he even knew when I was upset. He might not change to please me, but he knew.

"What, the end of the world isn't enough to be worried about?"

"It could be worse. We could still be in Reno." He shuddered. "I can't imagine what it is like."

"I'm not criticizing coming on this trip. I agree it was the right thing."

"Then what is bothering you."

I looked into his eyes and was so tempted to tell him how I felt. To be honest and lay it all out. About loving him. About how he was the most special person I had ever met. But, I hope I've given you the impression that I am not a particularly dumb person. So I kept my mouth shut and just shrugged.

"We've been lucky so far," I said. "The route has fewer people. The fish in the rivers. The Indian food distribution center, the right place at the right time. Very lucky."

Chase nodded in agreement. "Lucky unless you consider murderous RV campers, volcano eruptions, and oh yeah, flash floods. I guess it is all perspective."

"It could be worse. No one is hurt. We are all together. Be honest. Did you think we would get this far?"

He looked off into the distance then said, "I wasn't sure. I hoped so, but I wasn't sure."

We sat in silence for a minute then he said, "We're going to start hitting farm country in a couple of days. Towns, farms, people."

"What happens then?" I asked.

"I wish I knew," he said then added. "But whatever happens. We will be better off if we are well rested. You should get some sleep."

Staring out into the desert I turned to him and said, "Can I sleep out here? It's cooler."

He didn't laugh. Just motioned for me to lay down then draped a blanket over me. I snuggled in and held the blanket up to catch the strong smell I would always associate with Chase, wood smoke, leather, and sage.

Six hours later I woke in the warm embrace of heaven. Chase's hard chest against my back, his arm draped over me, holding me tight, making the world feel safe. Making me feel safe.

I think me waking woke him. I don't know how. But he was so attuned to everything around him, my simple change in breathing was enough to wake him from the deepest slumber.

Wiping his eyes he paused and studied me for a moment. My heart broke with want and need but I brought it under control and hurried to get up and wake the boys. "We need to get going," I told them, knowing if I turned back Chase would see me blushing and know how much I loved him.

Of course, my silly wants and wishes all disappeared two days later. We were walking down the middle of the road. Endless grasslands in all directions. The sun had just come up and the air was beginning to start heating up. The wind bringing in the future warm air that was going to make for a hot miserable day. I realized just how much I was going to miss air conditioning.

I had my head down as I thought about Chase and wondered how I could make him aware of my feelings without him knowing I had feelings. You know, stupid stuff when Chase suddenly cursed under his breath.

"What?" I asked as I looked up to see six men riding towards us. Each dressed in an army uniform.

Chapter Nineteen

<u>Chase</u>

I had known things were going too good. A nervous itch between my shoulder blades had been bugging me ever since we left Reno. Always waiting for the other shoe to fall. But like Meagan had said, we had been lucky.

Most of that could be laid at the feet of there being no people. We'd passed through an empty part of the country. It was spring, not the heat of summer. The asteroid's rain showers had helped. All of that was why we were lucky. There had been room to avoid problems. But that was about to end. I just knew it.

The four of us stood and waited for the soldiers to ride up. Two of them looked like they'd just learned how to ride. But the other four looked like they'd grown up on the back of a horse.

Dressed in camo, with side arms and rifles. The leader looked about twenty-five with three sergeant chevrons.

"Where you from?" he asked as he pulled his horse to a stop. His eyes quickly scanned us then moved past our group to scan the area, obviously looking for others.

I noticed two of the men had moved their rifles to sit across their laps, ready for use.

"Reno," I answered him. "Almost three weeks ago."

He winced, "You got out of there just in time."

I raised an eyebrow asking why.

"We got a radio working. Bicycle generated electricity. An old tube type. We're working on fixing some of the generators on the Snake River. But we got word. Reno is gone."

"What?" Meagan gasped.

"Yeah, I guess there was a big fight or something. But fires were started and there wasn't a fire department to put them out. So the place burned to the ground. Anyone who managed to live is wandering around the desert searching for their next meal."

I glanced over at Meagan and felt my heart break at the sorrow in her eyes. Her friends, schoolmates. But I couldn't spend time worrying about it now. Returning my attention to the soldier I said, "We're going up north of Elmira. My grandfather has a farm."

The soldier shook his head. "No, you're not. You're going to see Colonel Sullivan. He'll tell you what you're going to do."

I froze. God I hate being dictated to.

"Corporal Benson," he called over his shoulder. "The Corporal will escort you to the colonel. It's about five miles down the road. If you've walked from Reno, it will be easy." He then gestured at the desert and added. "Don't think about running. We'll get you before you can get too far. Besides, there isn't anywhere to run to."

He then waved his arm and the others followed him down the road. I thought about the Indian Reservation and wondered how things would work out when the Army tried to tell them what to do.

Some things never change.

The corporal, a big swede with a square head and fine blond hair smiled from the back of his horse then motioned for us to start walking.

I glanced over at Meagan then shrugged. The sergeant was right. There was nowhere to run to. That is the thing about the desert. Not a lot of places to hide.

The corporal walked his horse slowly, not even paying attention to us.

"What's the deal with this colonel?" I asked as I tried to map out our immediate future.

The man up on horseback smiled. "The colonel is the man. You do not want to mess with him."

"What's so special about him," Meagan asked, obviously wanting as much information as me.

"Martial Law," the soldier said. "That's what makes him the man. His word in these parts of Idaho is the law. Literally. They shot a man for stealing food. Firing squad and blindfold. Everything."

My stomach tightened. A man with too much power could mess with our plans.

"What's he like?" Meagan asked.

I shot her a quick smile, the girl was so intelligent, she saw what I saw, an obstacle that might need to be manipulated or overcome.

Corporal Beson smiled slyly then shrugged. "It isn't any secret. You'll learn soon enough. Strict, but fair. But ... he's a bible thumper. So I wouldn't curse, and don't try lying. That man can spot a lie at a thousand yards."

My mind scrambled to place him into a category as I tried to work out possible scenarios but I quickly realized I was working in the dark. I would have to wait and see.

"How bad has it been," Meagan asked, obviously enjoying speaking to someone other than her normal group.

The soldier smiled as he shrugged. Obviously enjoying speaking to a pretty girl. Again, some things never change.

I had to bite down on my back teeth. The look he gave her made me want to pull him off his horse. It wasn't creepy, but it was obvious he was interested. I couldn't blame him. But that didn't mean I was okay with it either.

"It's been bad," he said. "But not as bad as the rest of the country. You got fighting in some areas. I guess Missouri is in full-on civil war from what I hear. The city folk fighting with the country people over food. Granaries being overrun. Full-on battles. Same over in Spokane. Like the sergeant said, we have a working radio. There are some out there. HAMS, a couple of army units, people who got a solar system to work, or like us, bicycles, the transistors to our solar stuff is useless. New York is toast. Like Reno, they burned to the ground.

I thought of my sister, Haley. Please, I begged, please have escaped from there. My cousin Ryan, had he gotten away from the coast? And my cousin Cassie, Uncle Frank said she was down in Tulsa Oklahoma. Good, she should be safe there.

We both looked up at him hoping for more.

"They've opened some camps," he added. "for people without food. We're getting it to them. The camps, by wagons and horses. But everyone is worried about what is going to happen when we run out. No one is getting in a crop this year. Not like normal. Not enough to feed everyone."

He looked off into the distance with a sad smile. "They've put the state in lockdown. Only residents are allowed in. But we haven't had many people trying from this direction. Most have tried to come in from Spokane. My buddy said there were some trying from Montana, but not many. There aren't any big cities on that side."

"Lockdown?" I asked. "What does that mean exactly?" A nervousness filled me. Had we come all this way only to be turned away?

"Just what it sounds like. You've got to have ID with an Idaho address or you aren't allowed in."

Meagan gasped, then glanced over at me, obviously worried, her large eyes staring at me asking me what we were going to do.

All I could do was shrug. We'd fight that battle when we got there.

Two hours later we'd entered farming country with green fields irrigated by the Snake River. But like everywhere else, I could smell the green aroma of alfalfa and could only shake my head. We'd have beef for a while.

We entered a temporary army camp surrounded by barbed wire and the occasional watch tower. The four of us stared at each other then this new world. Endless rows of white tents stretched across a wide field. Large green tents forty or sixty feet long surrounded the camp. Cooking and administrative tents I assumed.

I shuddered. All these people. My worst nightmare. Or at least before that asteroid. My worst fear was being locked up with a thousand people. Now, here I was voluntarily walking into just such a world.

Corporal Benson led us through the armed gates to the only semi-permanent building in the camp. A doublewide trailer with the wheels still on. Off to the side was a large lean-to with six stationary bikes, each with a young man or woman pedaling.

The corporal saw me looking over at them and laughed, "The new Southern Idaho Power Company. They go directly into the batteries. No transistors or computers anywhere in the system. One hour of riding. We've got more than enough people. We need more of those bike generators."

I could only stare and marvel that we had been reduced to this and yet, I was thankful, it was the first step back from the dark ages.

Without getting down from his horse he passed us off to a barrel-chested First Sergeant with a name tag of Loy, who glared at us with beady eyes as if we were going to destroy his pristine camp. As we stood there, the corporal gave all of our details to the First Sergeant then pulled his horse around and galloped out of the camp probably back to his buddies down at the reservation.

The First Sergeant told us to drop our packs and hand over my pistol. "You'll get it back when you leave."

I hesitated, but really I didn't have a choice. He led us into the trailer and into a back room, A soft yellow light the only illumination. The first working lightbulb I'd seen in six weeks.

Coming to full attention, the First Sergeant said, "Sir, four outsiders just brought in from north of the Reservation. They say they left Reno three weeks ago."

A tall thin man with close-cropped silver hair was bent over a large desk covered in maps and papers. He frowned, obviously pulling himself out of his thoughts back to deal with this new situation. I could see it behind his eyes. The last thing he needed was more problems.

I saw the silver eagles on his collar and realized this must be the infamous Colonel Sullivan. He studied me for a long moment and I felt my insides tighten up. You did not want this man as an enemy.

"Are they on the list?" he asked the First Sergeant?"

"Chase Conrad is," he said, looking down at a clipboard, nodding to me. "Not the others."

My heart jumped. What list? How was I on a list?

Seeing my confusion. The colonel said, "Someone took the time to get your name onto the permission list. That means they hiked into some city and got ahold of someone important in time for the list to be sent out to all the army checkpoints. It's your lucky day. You get to come in."

Both Meagan and the boys sighed, obviously, they had been as worried as I had been.

The Colonel frowned then shook his head. "Only you Mr. Conrad. You and immediate family."

"What? No?" I gasped as my heart fell.

"Those are the rules. Or we'd be overrun."

I scoffed at the man. "Are you going to send a girl and two little boys back out into the desert? All alone?"

He glared at me, obviously not liking to be challenged then his eyes narrowed as he said, "If they are alone, it is because you abandoned them. I'm not stopping you from going back to where you came from. They just can't come in."

I glared back and realized he would do it. We stared at each other for the longest minute then he smiled slightly and said to the First Sergeant, "Go get the Chaplin, Please inform him I am in need of his services."

My first thought was that the Colonel was telling me I was going to need last rights in a few minutes if I didn't back down. Meagan saw it too and put a hand on my arm.

"No, Meagan," I said. "They can't keep us out."

The Colonel laughed. "As said by everyone who has tried and failed to get in. We have drawn a line. If I break it, everything falls apart. You can go back. The reservation might take you in. Or go a little south of them. Tuscarora maybe."

My jaw dropped. "You are sentencing them to death. You realize that don't you?"

He put both hands on his desk and leaned forward, his eyes bearing into me.

"Listen, kid. People are dying every day. No matter what we do, they die. We can't get food to them. Or they run out of medicine. And it's going to get worse. Every person I let in is one more that needs to be fed.

"But ..."

"No buts," he growled. "We have rules for a reason. Only people with an Idaho address or those who are on the lists and their immediate family. A line in the sand that can not be crossed or everything falls apart."

"But ..."

"No, those are the rules."

I felt my world begin to crumble as I realized I would never be able to change his mind. We would have to return to the desert. God, it was becoming early summer, if the heat didn't bake us, the lack of food or water would kill us.

Glancing over at Meagan I felt my world shake. Her face was as white as new snow. Both of the boys were looking at me, their eyes begging me to fix this. Even Shaina looked up at me, judging me, silently telling me that I was failing as a member of her pack.

My mind was scrambling, trying to figure out what we could do. We might try to sneak through somewhere else but I just knew we would fail. The country was flat and open. I

208

thought about the man they shot for stealing food. What was the punishment for sneaking into Idaho?

Suddenly there was a knock at the door followed immediately by the First Sergeant and another man stepping in. The Chaplin I assumed.

"You wished to see me, Sir?" he said to the Colonel.

The colonel nodded. "Yes, it seems we have a person on the list and a person not on the list. Really, there is only one answer. They have to get married."

Meagan gasped as she took a step back, almost fainting. James caught her. The look of pure terror on her face told me just how much she detested the idea. A man doesn't need much more to know where he stands.

Chapter Twenty

Meagan

Marry! The man expected me to marry Chase Conrad. Never. No. I couldn't do that to him. It wasn't right to ruin his life. "No," I said softly as I shook my head.

Chase frowned. As if I'd hurt him but quickly hid it then leaned in and whispered. "Don't worry. It won't be real. Once we get up north we'll get it annulled."

I looked back at him trying to understand.

He leaned in even closer, making my heart flutter. "Don't worry," he continued. "As long as we don't … you know. We can just cancel it. Who's going to stop us? I have to get to my grandfather's but I can't leave you guys."

Staring back at him I tried to make my mind work. Marry Chase? How had a secret dream become a nightmare? No, we couldn't

Chase stepped back then said to the Colonel. "We'll do it."

Everyone in the room looked at me, obviously waiting for my go-ahead. At least I had some say. But really, did I? If I didn't marry him it would mean the boys being sent back out into the desert. And I knew Chase, he would abandon his sanctuary, abandon his goal of getting to his family. He would come with us.

We would all die. Why? Because I refused to marry the greatest guy in the history of the world. Swallowing hard, I nodded. It was make-believe I told myself. I wouldn't ruin his life. It was only until we got to safety.

There were outs.

But my mind still refused to accept the reality of the situation as I was numbly moved into place. Austin and Shaina next to me. Jimmy on the other side of Chase.

The Chaplin started the proceeding but I was too numb to follow. How could this be happening? Twice he had to ask me if I took this man for my husband. I finally mumbled, "I do." Without really wanting to say the words.

A woman dreams about her wedding. Plans a thousand details. Family and friends. It was one of the most important days of her life. And this. This farce just was not the wedding I had hoped for.

And Chase. Poor Chase, being forced into this just to save us. Once again, placing us above his own well-being. For one thing, I knew with every fiber of my being. Chase Conrad did not want to be married to me. Boys like him didn't marry girls like me. The universe doesn't work that way.

Suddenly Chase held up a hand to stop the proceedings then raced out of the room. My heart fell. A secret dread of mine, being abandoned at the altar. Of course he was running away. But deep down, a sadness filled me. Not at the idea of being sent into the desert. No, a sadness at the realization that I had lost him.

Only I hadn't. He stepped back into the room, A smile a mile wide, holding up my grandmother's gold wedding band.

My heart melted. He'd saved it. He hadn't traded it to that farmer's wife.

Smiling, he slipped it on my finger then leaned forward to kiss me on the cheek.

A small part of me died at that moment. No long lingering kiss on the lips. But then I reminded myself this was not real. It didn't mean anything.

Glancing over at the Colonel I made sure to give him my best evil stare. I might be married, but I hadn't gotten what I wanted. A Chase who loved me. A Chase who wanted to be married to me.

"Sign here," The Colonel said as he turned a large green ledger book around to face us. "It's the unit log." He had written, *"Chase Conrad and Meagan Foster were married this day by Major Pulliver. Colonel Sullivan as witness."*

I looked down at the words and had to fight back a tear. Oh, how I wished they were true. Tightening my jaw I pushed myself to sign my name and had to stop and force myself to write Meagan Conrad.

We hadn't even discussed me taking his last name. I mean, sure, I would have done it in an instant if he had really wanted to marry me. I'd have done anything to earn his love. But I hadn't even been asked.

The Colonel looked down at our signatures then smiled. "Now everything is official. You can enter Idaho. You can even keep your dog. We're accepting working dogs and hunting hounds. Little dogs, no, they just take food. If you wish to stay here you will be given a tent.

"We will be staying," Chase said then quickly glanced over at me. "At least for a few days."

The Colonel called in the sergeant and told him to take us to our new tent. I was in a fog as we retrieved our packs and followed the sergeant. No one threw rice. No one wished us well, not even dirty jokes about the wedding night.

An emptiness filled me as I tried to pull myself up out of this black funk that was swallowing me.

Chase pointed to the barbed wire fence and asked, "You trying to keep people out or in?"

"Neither. It's an army base. We don't know how to live without a fence around us. And if you see stuff that doesn't make sense, just remember, it's the army. Half the stuff we do doesn't make sense."

The tents were laid out in a perfect grid over bare ground. Each with eight canvas cots.

"How many people?" Chase asked.

"Almost five thousand, a lot of them out of Twin Falls. But we're trying to set up food distribution in the city or we're going to get overrun."

"Where'd you get the food."

The sergeant smiled. "The first day. While everyone else was running around like chickens with their heads cut off. The Colonel. The first thing he did was seize all the food. The granaries, the warehouses. The supermarkets. He knew what was going to happen before most people even knew there was a problem."

I noticed Chase pursed his lip then nodded, obviously approving.

"Two meals a day," the sergeant said as he pulled a tent flap back and waved us into an empty tent with the eight cots, "They serve breakfast early. Don't be late or you'll go hungry. It's up to you if you want to save any for your lunch. Someone will let you know your work assignments tomorrow."

Before we could ask any more he turned and left us. I swallowed hard as I looked at the cots. Chase caught me staring then gently touched my arm. "Don't worry. It's just another day. None of that stuff mattered."

I looked at him and couldn't take it anymore a lone tear spilled over and began to crawl down my cheek. When I saw the pain in his eyes I lost it even more and pushed past him before I became a blubbering fool.

A thousand emotions rushed through me. Not just the world ending and six weeks of endured pain and misery. A life of misery. A dead father who hadn't walked me down the aisle. A mother in prison who hadn't helped me plan my wedding. All my friends died in the fires of Reno. A world gone to hell in a thousand different ways. All of it was just too much.

Collapsing behind a tent I buried my head in my knees and held on as ugly tears poured out of me.

"Hey honey," someone said behind me. "Are you all right?"

Gulping I took a long breath and forced myself to try and regain some respectability. I turned to find an older woman about my grandmother's age which made me want to start crying all over.

"I didn't want to interrupt," she said. "But. I ... well, I'm here if you need anything."

My heart melted. Even in the worst of times. Some people were just plain nice. Suddenly I had to tell someone. "It's my wedding day." I managed to say around the last of my sobs.

She frowned then smiled sadly. "I would say I'm sorry. But I don't know why."

I laughed. "Because he doesn't love me. We were forced to marry. So that I and my brothers could get into Idaho."

She frowned trying to understand so I told her my entire story. Getting into the wreck, Chase walking out of the forest all handsome and hot. Saving me and my brothers over and over. Always so sweet. My grandmother making him stay against his will.

"So let me get this right," she said, "You're married to a nice, handsome man who has repeatedly demonstrated both bravery and intelligence. And you like him."

I scoffed. "That is putting it mildly. I love him, with all my heart."

She smiled sweetly then said, "Oh honey. Every woman wishes to have your problems.

You're young, beautiful, married to a good man. It doesn't get better than that. Not in this world."

My heart broke, she didn't understand. "It is not real. It's all pretend."

Her smile widened, "Until it isn't."

Patting my arm, she gave me one last smile then left me to my misery. Eventually, I realized I was going to have to go back and face Chase and my brothers. But of course, when I stepped into the tent all three of them were asleep on cots. My problems obviously didn't mean anything. Shaina was the only one to wake up and give me a quick tail wag before laying on her side.

I did notice that Chase had put my backpack at the foot of the cot next to his. My heart broke again as I realized I desperately wanted to move it next to him. To snuggle up and share our wedding night at least holding hands.

But instead, I laid down and forced myself to sleep.

The next morning I woke to find Chase shooting me a quick smile. But no one brought up my crying jag from the day before. Instead, they were all hopping around waiting for me.

We visited the latrines. Port-a-potties, then went into breakfast. We grabbed the metal trays and joined the long line.

For the first time, I started to look at the people. A lot of older people. I realized. Why? A few women with little kids. People were quiet, no jovial joshing. No fighting. Suddenly I realized. People were afraid of being kicked out of the camp.

What must it have been like, watching your food slowly disappear? Only to be offered this salvation.

Breakfast consisted of a thick chunk of bread and a bowl of oatmeal with a dash of syrup for sweetness. We sat at a table. I noticed most people leaned over their bowl, their arms surrounding it as if terrified someone would take it from them.

Chase shook out his paper napkin then wrapped his piece of bread in it. "For lunch," He told the boys who quickly followed his example.

"But we have food in our packs."

"Shush," he hissed holding a finger to his lips then turning to see if anyone heard. "We'll save that for the road."

After breakfast, the sergeant showed up and gave us our job assignments. I was given the kitchen clean-up detail. I was about to complain about the gender role assignments but then he gave Chase the latrine clean-up duties and I realized I had gotten off on the easier side.

Jimmy was sent off to help with the cattle in a far pen and Austin was to take Shaina and report to the shepherd. I would learn they had about a hundred sheep just outside the camp.

I balked at the idea of him being so far away. The sergeant smiled. "He'll be safe. Your dog wouldn't let anything happen to him. And the shepherd is cool. I promise."

I looked over at Chase and knew he was thinking about our fight over Jimmy going off on his own. Yes, the boys needed to grow into their independence. But now? Here?

"I'll be fine," Austin told me. "I'll bet the sheep are next to the cows. Jimmy can walk me over."

So that is how we spent our first day in the camp. And the second and the third. Working long hours, but being fed. Not a lot, but enough. And because we weren't walking twenty miles a day. I could see the calories adding weight back onto the boys in only a couple of days. They were losing that skinny look.

We would meet for dinner meal. Usually a soup and two pieces of bread. They had made some accommodations. Children were given one cup of milk per day. Jimmy told us about the four dairy cows they had and how he'd held their heads while they were milked.

The milk still had the cream and was packed with calories.

Austin told us how pleased the shepherd was with Shaina. That she didn't know anything but was a quick learner. He couldn't stop talking about how the man had shown him how to train the dog. "She's smart," he had said. "So basically she'll end up training you. But she's good with the sheep. Knows how to keep them in line."

On the third day, Chase was moved off latrine duty to butchering duty and spent the day helping butcher a steer. Again I didn't complain about my clean-up duties.

As I scrubbed the trays and bowls I noticed there were almost never any leftovers to scrape into a slop can. But I was usually able to get enough to feed Shaina each night. Another reason not to complain about my assignment.

So we were busy. The woman who had sat with me during my crying fiasco was named Beth Harding and she made it a point of becoming my friend. Joking, always asking if I was doing okay. We were sitting at our evening meal when she saw me and came over. I introduced her and noticed she spent a long minute examining Chase before she leaned down and whispered, "I understand." Then shot me a quick smile before leaving us.

"What was that all about?" Chase asked.

"Nothing," I said as I waved my hand in dismissal. Trying not to blush.

We were doing well. Our bodies were recovering. I was able to get new shoes for the boys. Or at least good previously owned shoes. They'd outgrown the ones we left home with. That and walked the souls off of them.

I noticed they didn't even mention the brand. No complaining about not having the latest Nike. Nope. All that stuff went out the window the day the asteroid hit.

They had showers, with actual almost warm water. We were allowed one per week. Women and men on separate days. As I allowed the water to rinse out my shampoo I couldn't stop from remembering walking out of the lake and being caught by Chase. Naked. I remembered the look in his eyes.

Why couldn't he look at me like that now? We were married.

But overall, we were doing well and could leave anytime we wanted. As the Sergeant said. They wanted us to leave. Less people to feed. Less problems. But Chase said he wasn't ready yet. I don't know what he was waiting for but I could see something going on in the back of his mind. A plan was coming together.

So we were doing well. But beneath it all was a tension between me and Chase. We hadn't discussed our marriage. Hadn't dealt with anything. It was like a huge rock on the edge of a cliff ready to fall and kill us all.

What did he think about it? I mean did it make him shudder or cringe? Did the idea of being married to me fill his mind with regret and shame? I mean what if he met someone else? The camp was filled with pretty girls and I'd seen more than one shooting Chase glances. The fact that he didn't have a wedding band of his own irked me to the tenth degree.

What would happen if he wanted to marry someone else but he was held back by me and the signatures on a page? Were we to just pretend it hadn't happened? And how could we get it annulled? Who did that in this new world? I mean would we have to find an army person somewhere? But if we did, did that mean I would have to leave the state?

Suddenly I realized we might not be able to get the marriage annulled. Not and keep my brothers safe. Suddenly I realized I really had ruined Chase's life.

Chapter Twenty-Two

<u>Chase</u>

The camp wasn't too bad. Us civilians were given the dirty jobs. The soldiers waltzed around with their weapons making sure things stayed quiet. But they were stuck here. We could leave any time we wanted. I'd already seen two families pick up and take off. So I didn't have to worry about that anymore. The boys were doing well and Meagan seemed like she was accepting things.

My heart ached remembering the look of fear on her face when she was told she was going to have to marry me. The idea of hurting her was out of bounds in my book. But there hadn't been an option.

That didn't take the sting away though. So I threw myself into work and spent as little time around her as possible. I refused to add to her stress.

But I will admit, at night, the smell of her shampoo, hearing her breath in her cot two feet away, was driving me crazy. I would wake in the morning and stare across the divide at her, sleeping innocently, and feel my heart break. Two feet away, and on the other side of the world.

After we had been there for a week the first Seargent collared me and told me to report to the main gate for food detail.

When I got there I discovered five wagons, each drawn by four horses, a man atop each seat with reins in their hands. A dozen soldiers on horseback, each with their weapons drawn like they were expecting World War Three.

"Jump up," someone yelled. "We don't have all day."

I climbed up to sit next to a guy in his mid-twenties who kept glancing at the horses nervously, the reins bunched in his hand.

"Do you know how to drive a wagon?" I asked.

He shook his head. "They told me what to do."

I laughed and took the reins from his hands, separating them so I could interlace the left reins through my left fingers then the same for the right. "My grandfather taught me before he taught me how to drive the tractor." I sighed as I remembered his huge hands being so gentle. God, I hoped the old man was alright. I couldn't imagine a world without him in it.

The man sighed, his shoulders slumping in relief. "I tried to tell them."

"My name's Chase," I said as I examined the horses. They looked good and stood ready to go. Obviously, they'd been trained to pull wagons. Six weeks into this disaster and we were starting back. Of course, I thought about those wild mustangs and wondered if they'd be pulling a wagon next year.

"Joel," he answered, "Joel Barns."

I was about to ask where we were going when a soldier yelled and the first wagon began to move. I flicked the reins and felt a thousand memories fill my mind as the horses tugged the empty wagon.

It was easy to keep them on the road, they simply followed the wagon in front. We passed through farm country and green fields with the Snake River off to the left.

It got so boring that Joel and I exchanged stories. He and his family were from Twin Falls. "We weren't ready," he said with a shake of his head. "Marla was a stay-at-home mom. I was working two jobs. Driving a cement truck during the day and working at the liquor store at night. Truck driver and clerk. Not exactly in high demand anymore.

He looked off into the distance. "Even with two jobs, we never had enough. When this hit. I could see what was going to happen. People got afraid. And the liquor store." He shook his head. "I was there the night we got raided. Money didn't work. The credit card system. And people wanted their booze. I don't think Colonel Sullivan and his battalion could have stopped those looters."

I nodded, encouraging him to continue.

He shrugged. "We held out for six weeks. Marla, me, and the two kids. But we ran out of food. I heard about the camps. Really, we didn't have a choice."

I told him about Reno and making it out in time and the long walk we endured.

We talked about before the asteroid and what we thought the future would look like. He was a nice guy, smart, dedicated father and husband. And terrified about what was going to happen to his family.

Finally, we were all talked out and simply continued on until I noticed two half circles of sandbags six feet high each with a .50 caliber machine gun covering the surrounding area. Two more on the other side of the nine tall grain silos. The soldiers behind the guns looked serious.

Obviously, Colonel Sullivan had secured all this food and meant to keep it that way.

I glanced over at Joel and said, "I guess this stuff is important."

He swallowed hard.

We were directed into a gravel yard and told to tie off the horses then help fill bags. Ten men, all civilians, scrambled down to the second silo. The soldiers took up positions around the perimeter like they were expecting to be attacked by a Mongolian horde or something. Someone turned a wheel, lifting a door and wheat shished out of the silo onto the ground.

The soldiers kept watch while we filled burlap bags with the grain. Joel and I took turns with the shovel or holding the bag. It took us over an hour to fill a hundred bags. And another hour to load the wagon.

I noticed the soldiers where supper alert on the trip back.

Joel said, "It's like we're transporting gold."

"It's worth more," I said as I flicked the reins to keep the horses moving. They were laboring pulling two tons of wheat but we didn't have far to go.

I was pleased to see Meagan standing by the front gate waiting for me. Did she care? Had she missed me? Or was something wrong?

She shot me a quick smile, silently letting me know everything was okay. I pulled the wagon in next to the food tent tied off the reins and jumped down to give her a quick hug.

"I ... we missed you," she said and I noticed a blush.

I nodded as the hostlers came to get the horses and a dozen people started unloading the bags of wheat.

She slipped her arm into mine and said, "They said it was dangerous. That people might try to take the food."

I laughed. "The Army outguns them. Even people around here don't have machine guns."

Pulling her around I was going to introduce her to Joel when I noticed a new set of soldiers holding their horses. It took me a minute to believe what I was seeing.

"Tim?" I asked.

A young soldier with corporal's stripes turned and stared until he recognized me. A smile a mile wide broke across his face. "Conrad. You evil bastard. I knew you'd make it."

I dropped Meagan's arm so that I could pound Tim on the back. "What are you doing here? And in the army?"

He gripped my hand and shook his head. "I saw Ryan and Haley. They both made it."

"What? Really?" Wow. I turned to Meagan, "My sister, my cousin. Tim says he saw them."

She smiled, then glanced at Tim, obviously confused.

"Meagan, this is Tim Devo. My fishing buddy, hunting partner, and worst liar in north Idaho."

Tim smiled at her and I saw the immediate interest in his eyes. I'm rather proud that I didn't punch him. Instead, I said, "Tim, this is my wife, Meagan."

Tim's jaw dropped.

Meagan spun to stare at me, obviously surprised at how I had introduced her.

"Wife?" Tim said as he shook his head. "Ryan had a girlfriend. Haley a boyfriend. A big guy. But wife. Leave it to you. You never did anything half way. I guess my putting your guys' names on the list worked.

I stared at him, "It was you?"

He shrugged. "Somebody had to."

I couldn't believe Tim Devo was standing here telling me about Haley and Ryan. It was surreal. "Why are you here?" I asked him.

He smiled. "We're here to escort this food up to Boise."

"That's a long way," I said. "And there is a ton of farms up that way. More than down here."

He shrugged. "Then we're taking the wagons on to Coeur d'Alene. I think they want the wagons more than the food. It's the army, don't try and figure them out."

I laughed as a sudden thought hit me. We both froze as the same idea occurred to us each. "Would they?" I asked.

"Maybe," he replied. "You can drive a wagon. That puts you ahead of almost everyone else in line. Plus, You have a good reference. The Lieutenant listens to me."

Meagan looked at me then him then back to me asking for an explanation.

"How would you and the boys like to ride to Coeur d'Alene? It beats walking."

Her eyes widened as she began to understand.

"Can you ask?" I asked him. "There are four of us, Two young boys, Meagan's brothers. And a dog."

He frowned for a moment then shrugged. "I'll ask. How about I find you in the dinner tent in about an hour? I'll let you know."

"Great," I said then slipped my arm around Meagan and kissed her on the cheek. She froze, looking up at me like I was some alien from another planet. "Come on, Let's talk to the boys."

She didn't pull away from me. Obviously not wanting to be disrespectful in front of my friend. But I did feel a tenseness in her body as if she despised being held like this.

When we were out of sight of Tim she pulled out from under my arm and glared at me. "What was that all about?"

"Tim?"

231

"No, you treating me like a wife. You haven't said three words to me for a week. You've been avoiding me. Now, your friend shows up and you're all over me."

I froze and almost tripped over a tent post. "I didn't want him getting any ideas."

Her frown deepened. "Ideas?"

"Yeah, you know. You're taken."

"Taken?" she asked as she put her hands on her hips. "But it's all pretend, you idiot. Remember."

My heart broke a little. Obviously, I'd overstepped. "I'm sorry. I won't do it again," I snarled as I stomped off.

Meagan stood there staring daggers into my back as if I'd killed her favorite cat.

Nope, I wouldn't make that mistake again. In fact, the sooner we got up north the better. Then she could go her way and I could go mine. Like she said, it was all pretend.

Chapter Twenty-Three

<u>Meagan</u>

It was so wrong. This desperately lonely feeling sitting next to Chase. He hadn't apologized. Not really. And if I'm honest I don't know what I wanted him to apologize for. I just knew I needed him to.

We were both sitting up on the wagon seat. Just like everything he did, he was an excellent wagon driver. One more thing for me to be mad about. His damn perfection. Both of the boys and Shaina were in the back sitting on the bags of wheat along with our backpacks.

The morning air was crisp with the sun rising off to our right. I glanced over at Chase from the corner of my eyes and ground my teeth. "Is it going to be like this all the way there?" I asked.

"Like what?"

Fighting to not roll my eyes I took a deep breath, "The two of us not talking."

He scoffed and flicked the reins reminding me once again I wasn't his priority. "I didn't know we were not talking. Now that I know, I'll try to accommodate your desires."

"Chase," I snapped. "Don't be a jerk."

He shrugged. "Hey, it's better than being an idiot."

I cringed as my words were thrown back at me. Taking a deep breath I closed my eyes and counted to ten. When I was done, I looked over at Chase and hated the idea of us fighting. We weren't like that. And I didn't even know why we were fighting. I didn't know what to fix, let alone how.

He glanced at me then quickly came back at the horses.

"You're not an idiot," I said, "I am sorry for calling you that."

He sighed and said, "I'm sorry for getting all possessive."

My heart broke. I wanted him to be possessive. I wanted him to think I was the only girl in the world. But I wanted it for real, not fake. Not to show off in front of his friend. Not if it wasn't real.

I wanted real, I realized, more than anything in this world. I wanted real. But being the smart girl I am, I pressed my lips together and shut up before I made a major fool of myself.

"So," he started. "Are we done fighting?"

I laughed. "I guess so."

He nodded then turned back to the boys in the back. "I want you guys to move the bags, create a fort for you to hide in the middle. Make enough room for your sister."

I frowned up at him and he shook his head. "This food is the most valuable thing around. Someone might want to take it. Why do you think we have a dozen soldiers guarding it? If the shooting starts, you jump into the back with the boys. Those bags of grain will abord most shots."

I couldn't believe him. Not really. But I still made sure the boys created a high barrier to hide behind.

We stopped at noon to water the horses and give them a rest. Chase's friend, Tim, rode back from scouting in front to the column and reported to the lieutenant then trotted back to us. He shot me a quick smile then nodded when he saw the fort the boys had made.

"It's all clear for the next ten miles. We'll camp on the other side of the Snake."

I could only nod and realized just how not in control I was. I felt like a piece of driftwood floating along in a river. Going where the current took me. No agency.

This is how you end up in a pretend marriage to a boy who didn't want to be around you. A boy who was constantly sacrificing himself for you and your brothers. It was enough to make a girl want to scream in frustration.

Besides being frustrated. I was bored. At least when we were walking, I felt like we were doing something.

That evening we camped near the river. "We'll have to share the tent," Chase informed us. "There's nowhere to set up the tarp and I'm pretty sure it's going to rain tonight."

Was that because he didn't want anyone thinking we weren't a normal couple? I nodded. Again, what was I going to do? Say no?

The army gave us each a MRE. One of their packaged meals. I got spaghetti but traded with Jimmy for his stroganoff.

We were sitting around our own campfire when Tim came up and plopped down next to me. I glanced over at Chase, suddenly worried about a repeat of last time. I wouldn't overreact, I promised myself, and smiled at Tim.

"So," he began. "I've got to ask. What do you see in this idiot."

I cringed at his choice of words but then I smiled sweetly and said. "OH, just you know, the regular. Brave. Smart, Kind, and oh yeah, he makes my toes curl. Just the normal perfect guy stuff."

Tim laughed then glanced over at Chase. But Chase was staring at me like I'd just chopped the head of a snake and popped it in my mouth.

I ignored him. Liking the shocked look on his face. Suddenly I realized I desperately wanted to know what he was like growing up so I asked Tim to tell me stories.

He smiled and said, "I thought you'd never ask. I've been waiting to tell these for years."

Chase coughed and shook his head. "Remember. I've got just as many on you. Most of them worse."

Tim laughed. "Yeah, but I'm not married to a beautiful woman who thinks I'm special. She needs to know the truth."

"You're not married now. But someday. You know how this goes. I always give as good as I get."

I watched the two of them banter back and forth and realized just how close they were. Good friends who trusted each other implicitly.

Tim thought for a minute then shook his head and said, "You're lucky there's kids around. I'll only tell the clean ones."

Glancing over at my brothers I realized that both of them were being exceptionally quiet. Desperate to not draw attention to themselves and be sent away from the grown-up conversation.

Chase laughed but I could see the relief in his eyes. I made a promise to myself to corner Tim sometime in the future. A time when we were alone and get those stories out of him.

"How did you guys meet."

Tim smiled. "Our grandfathers were friends. My grandfather was half Nimiipuu, Nez Pierce. He and Chase's Papa served together in Viet Nam."

"They were on the same fire team, spent months together in foxhole talking about Idaho. Papa's sons moved away after college."

Tim nodded. "So when Chase and his family started spending the summers with their Papa, Mr. Conrad. I was asked to show them around."

"Tim's probably the best tracker, ever," Chase said with obvious admiration. "I thought I was good, But I swear he could track a bird flying over bare rock in a snowstorm."

Smiling, Tim said, "Chase, Ryan, his cousin, and I would spend half the summer camping out in the forest. Sometimes the girls, Cassie and Haley would tag along. Most Christmas breaks they'd come up."

"It really was a pretty great life," Chase said with obvious fondness. "Until ..." he added ominously.

Tim's head dropped. "Until I got a crush on Haley."

"Chase's sister?" I asked, loving the whole soap opera feel to everything.

Chase glared at Tim. "The only time we got into a knockdown drag-out fight."

"Who won?" Jimmy asked then immediately slammed his mouth closed.

"Neither of us," Chase said. "But we were both so bloody and bruised up it took a week to get right again. And it ruined the whole summer."

Tim shook his head. "You should see the guy she's with now. He's the size of a small mountain. And loves her more than life itself. You won't be getting between them. I promise. I know, I tried, and she about bit my head off."

Chase smiled thinking about his sister and knowing she was okay.

My heart ached, I wanted what she had. A man she loved loving her back.

A silence fell over us as we each thought about our new lives. What might have been and wondering what would now be?

Finally, large rain drops started hissing as they hit the fire. Chase announced it was time for bed and started kicking dirt over the fire. We each made one last trip to the bushes then I climbed into the tent. Both boys had taken one side, meaning Chase and I would have to sleep next to each other.

I was about to make them move when Chase pulled the flap back and shot me a look telling me to hurry. I snuggled down next to Jimmy and Chase got in behind me. The tent was too small, but we didn't have a choice.

I could feel him behind me. Breathing. The smell of leather and woodsmoke engulfed me. Surrounding me. Making me want to crawl into his arms and just be held.

But, I'm a big girl. And kept my hands to myself. When I woke that morning, I was disappointed to discover him already up and out of the tent. I had so hoped to have him surround me.

Pushing back a tear, I woke the boys and stepped outside to discover Chase squatting next to the fire, feeding it sticks with a pot of coffee bubbling. The sky had that early morning purple to gray look it gets about a half hour before sunrise.

He shot me a strange look that I couldn't begin to fathom then announced that we should hurry and grab some breakfast from the army guys because we were headed out soon.

One of the soldiers had scrambled some powdered eggs and there was two-day old bread.

Chase got the horses hooked up and hurried so he could be first in line when we left. He leaned over and smiled at me. "We won't be eating other people's dust."

I shook my head, he thought of everything, as always. Of course he wasn't smart enough to realize how I felt, and I wasn't lucky enough for him to feel the same way. I made a point of ensuring there was no tenseness between us. I asked for stories about Tim. About his grandfather. About his family. Anything to keep him talking.

I asked him to show me how to drive the wagon. He was about to give me the reins when the lieutenant held up his hand for the column to stop. I looked up and froze. A dozen men had rushed out onto the road. Each of them holding a rifle. Another dozen lined the forest on either side.

Gaunt, skinny men and boys. Each with a rifle.

"Get in the back," Chase hissed as he pushed both sets of reins into his left hand then pulled his pistol from its holster and laid it on the seat next to him. "Now," he barked, not taking his eyes off the men in front of him.

I swallowed hard then crawled over the back of the seat into the boy's fort where I pushed them down. My heart raced as I realized what was happening. Where we about to die? Had we come this far only to be killed by bandits?

Sitting up I looked over the back of the wagon seat, desperate to know what was happening.

"We'll be taking the wagons," A large man said, hands on his hips, the only man without a rifle.

"Corporal Devo," The lieutenant yelled as he held up his hand. Suddenly a soldier rode up next to each wagon and held a grenade over the wheat.

"One shot," the lieutenant said, "And we'll burn it all. We've got a can of gas in the middle of each wagon to burn it all. You won't get one seed."

I gulped as I looked up at the soldier. He was staring at the lieutenant, waiting for the word. Would he do it? Would he give us time to get out before he burned everything to the ground?

Shifting, I started at the man in the road and at the dozen men behind him and then the other along the side of the road in the bushes and behind some trees. I could see the fear in their eyes. They weren't terrified of being killed. They were terrified of losing all that food. Of seeing it wasted.

The lieutenant's horse shifted under him, and I thought he was going to drop his hand. The soldiers would react and everyone would die, But he steadied the horse with his knees then said, "You have ten seconds to get out of the way or it all goes up and we start shooting."

The leader glared up at the lieutenant then sighed heavily and motioned for his men to step back.

I sighed with relief. We weren't all going to die in a ball of fire. At least not right then.

The lieutenant shifted to look over his shoulder. "Give them ten bags," he told Corporal Devo. He then turned to Chase and motioned for him to go forward.

The soldiers rode along side the wagons ready to burn them if they were attacked. Tim had a soldier unload ten bags onto the road off the last wagon.

Chase kept flicking the reins making sure the horses didn't stop. Only when all the wagons were past did we all let out a long sigh of relief and the soldiers backed off from holding a grenade over us.

I climbed back up next to Chase to find him scowling.

"I shouldn't have brought you and the boys," he grumbled.

Laughing, happy to be alive I reached over and gave him a quick hug. "It wouldn't be right to leave your wife behind. Even if she is only pretend."

His scowl softened just a little before he smiled and shook his head. I didn't know what that meant but at least we weren't fighting anymore.

Chapter Twenty-Four

Chase

It took us three days to reach Boise. I honestly think we could have made it in two if we'd been walking but the horses were pulling two tons of wheat and needed hourly rests and early stops each night.

When we hit Boise, we rode through the center of town to a park. The Army had set up a barbed wire fence around the park and was actively patrolling. Only soldiers were inside so this wasn't a people-type camp.

After we finished unloading the bags of wheat the Lieutenant returned and told us to put ten bags back into my wagon. I didn't ask why, but I made a point of lining them up for protection. It wasn't enough but it was better than nothing.

I had to standby while the horses were reshod by an army farrier. But once they were all set, I returned to my group.

Meagan and I spent the early evening walking around Boise, trying to get some idea of how things were going. This was the first city we'd hit since leaving Reno. My heart broke when I saw the thin people waiting in line at an army soup kitchen.

The kids were the worst. It had been five weeks, and they were already looking gaunt. We really hadn't realized how much food it takes to keep a person fed. One of those things that goes on in the background that no one every thinks about.

We came across a small market. People had brought out tables, piling them high with items. They reminded me of a drive-in swap meet. Only here, it really was swap. No money exchanged hands.

Obviously, people were looking for food and had pulled out their prize possessions, hoping to get something. We watched as a can of peaches was traded for a chain saw. The old-fashioned kind that still worked. And I know some people would think the man getting the peaches got the better deal.

Meagan grabbed my hand and pulled me towards three folding tables piled high with clothes. "You need shirts,"

I scoffed. "What are we going to buy them with, Your good looks."

"No this," she said as she started to pull off her grandmother's wedding band.

"Stop," I hissed as my hand flashed out to stop her.

She frowned up at me. "Why not? It's just pretend, remember?"

I growled deep in my throat. How could I explain it to her? I didn't understand it myself. But I just didn't want her to. Instead, I pulled my pistol and removed one bullet. I would reload from the box in my backpack when we got back to the wagon.

Holding it up, I showed the vendor and said, "For five shirts. T-shirts or Polo."

Meagan gasped at my ridiculous asking price. But the seller, a woman in her early forties scrunched her brow then held up three fingers.

"Three bullets?" I gasped as I began to walk away.

"No, three shirts," she said, calling me back.

Smiling at Meagan, I asked her to pick them out then handed over the single bullet. Wow, the concept of value had certainly changed.

That night around the campfire, I noticed Meagan twirling her wedding band around her finger, lost in thought.

My heart broke. When we got to my grandfather's, she was going to insist we stop this charade of a marriage. She would want the opportunity to choose her own husband. The thought hit me like a ton of bricks. I didn't want her walking out of my life. She and the boys had become my number one priority, and I wouldn't know what to do with myself without them.

I felt my jaw drop as the realization hit me. I was desperately in love with Meagan Foster. No, in like. Full on in love.

Slowly, I pushed myself back to reality and pulled this new discovery out, and examined it from every detail. Why? Obviously, the girl was beautiful. With a sweet innocence that pulled at a man's soul. But there was her bravery. The way she stood up to me when she thought I was in the wrong. Her toughness. All the way across the desert, she'd never complained, never second guessed our decisions.

I loved to hear her laugh. Especially at my attempted humor. The way she'd flick her hair over her shoulders was heart-stopping. So many things.

There was the way she treated her brothers. With obvious love, but an insistence on discipline. Always concerned about their future, short-term, and down the road. What kind of men they would grow up to be?

She would be a good mom, I realized as my heart hurt. Desperately wanting her to be the mother of my children.

But most of all it was the peace she brought into my world. Things just felt better around her.

Looking up from twirling her ring she caught me staring at her.

"What?" she asked as her face suddenly blushed.

I was about to say something when Tim stepped into the firelight and squatted down to take my coffee cup out of my hands and pour himself a cup. He took a sip, wincing at the hot coffee then winked at Meagan.

She laughed. Obviously, the two of them loved poking at me.

"I'm taking off in the morning," Tim said, shooting me a quick glance. "I'm riding dispatches to the camp we've got over on the east side. They don't have a working radio. Twisted pair phone lines between the camp and the border. But no radio, not yet."

I nodded.

"We'll miss you," Meagan said, and I could see it in her eyes. She meant it. But it was an innocent look, not a flirty look that would have set me off.

Tim shrugged, then said, "I've talked to the lieutenant, you can drive all the way to Coeur d'Alene, but they've got to turn the wagons over when they get there, and you are on your own from that point forward."

I nodded. "Thanks, that will be great." We got to ride instead of walk. And we would be surrounded by soldiers. No one was going to mess with us. Plus, we didn't have enough food to justify attacking the group.

"Will you stay on the east side? If you do. I think that is the way Cassie would come in."

Tim frowned. "Why would she leave Oklahoma? That's a long walk and we don't have anything they don't have down there."

I shrugged. "I don't know. But keep an eye out for her, please."

He nodded. "No problem. Cassie was always the best out of you Conrads."

The next morning, Tim stuffed his saddlebags with letters then saluted the lieutenant. He then spun, gave Meagan a quick salute, and spurred his horse.

"We're back to the Pony Express," Meagan said as she shook her head with obvious sadness. "Wagons and post riders."

I watched Tim race away, bent over his horse's neck, and knew he was loving life. Living a life of adventure. Never knowing what would happen tomorrow. Doing important things for important people.

Glancing over at Meagan I suddenly realized if by some miracle we were able to make this marriage real I would be giving up any chance for such a life. I would be settled with one woman for the rest of my life. I'd be tied to our home and spend every day fighting to get enough to keep her and our family alive.

There would be no adventure. No long hikes through unknown country with no destination and no goal. My natural wanderlust would have to be wrestled to the ground and dispatched to history.

I would be saddled with responsibility for others. My worth would be judged by their happiness. I waited for the sadness to hit me. For shock and denial to wash over me.

But nothing happened except a small thrill at the thought of taking it all on. Yes, this was now the life I wanted. I would find meaning in making Meagan's life better. Without thinking, I reached out to take her hand and squeezed. I then took a deep breath and flicked the reins.

Meagan stared at me, wondering what was going on in my stupid brain. I just smiled at her as I began to figure out ways to make her fall in love with me.

It was almost four hundred miles along the western foothills of the Bitterroot mountains then another fifty up to my grandfather's place. I had a month to convince her that I was worth something.

So of course it became impossible. I could never get enough alone time. Between her brothers. The responsibility for the wagon, and the other soldiers, we were always surrounded by people. Too many people.

I had to sit next to her all day and keep my thoughts to myself. Smell the soap she'd gotten back in camp. A vanilla, coconut blend that ripped my soul in two.

We were three weeks into the trip when I thought the tension between us would make me spontaneously combust when she looked over her shoulder at her sleeping brothers, Shaina between them.

Glancing at me she smiled sadly.

"What?" I asked quietly.

She just shrugged and then proceeded to twist her wedding band.

I wondered if she even knew she was doing it. She did it whenever she became worried about something.

Taking a deep breath I let it out slowly and asked, "Meagan, what is bothering you?"

She grimaced then shook her head.

My left-wheel horse tossed his head and wanted to stop. I flicked the reins and clicked my tongue to keep him going. We'd stop soon. "We're almost there," I told him encouragingly.

He twitched his ears, but he kept pulling.

When we camped that night, I made sure he got an extra helping of oats then joined Meagan and the boys at our fire.

The soldiers were either on guard duty or playing cards. The Lieutenant was reading a map, holding it up to the fire to catch the light.

Meagan rose when I stepped in next to our fire, she suddenly grabbed my hand and indicated I should follow her.

I am not an idiot. Contrary to what some people might say. When a pretty girl invites you to follow her into the dark. You do it. Plain and simple.

A full moon and a starry night allowed us to move about with no problems. We passed the soldier on guard. He waved, acknowledging us then turned to give us some privacy. We wove our way down next to the creek and around a bend.

I wondered what this was all about but again, I just shut up before I ruined anything by talking and saying something dumb. Some famous guy said, better to be silent and thought a fool than speak and remove all doubt.

Finally, Meagan pointed to a patch of grass and said, "We need to talk."

My gut tightened, that sounded ominous. I wondered what I'd done wrong this time as I pulled up every memory for the last three days.

She sat down, pulling her legs up and wrapping her arms around them like girls do.

I sat down next to her and raised an eyebrow. This was her show.

She suddenly frowned then stared off into the night, her fingers instantly worrying her wedding band.

Letting out a long breath, she asked, "We should be in Coeur d'Alene tomorrow or the next day. Then we walk to your grandfather's. What two or three days away? What happens when we get there?"

My brow furrowed in confusion. "Why?"

She swung around to stare at me, her brow fixed in a serious frown. "I can't do this anymore. I need to know what is going to happen."

My confusion shot up about six degrees. "I can't tell you what's going to happen tomorrow. Let alone a week from now."

"Never mind," she snapped as she pushed herself up.

My heart broke at the thought of her storming off, angry at me for some reason that I couldn't begin to fathom. "Meagan, stop," I said as I took her hand.

She paused, looking down at my hand holding hers.

This was the moment, I realized. The moment when I had to tell her the truth. She was right. We needed to start making plans and we couldn't do that until the truth was out.

"Listen, there is something I have to tell you."

She looked up at me, waiting, I could see it in her eyes. Hope. The kind of look a girl gives a guy to let him know he can admit the truth and she won't laugh in his face.

"You know how special you are," I began, still too terrified to say the actual words.

She simply raised an eyebrow, silently insisting I actually say the words.

"I ..."

"Halt ..." Somebody yelled from the darkness behind us then the night erupted in gunfire. Yellow explosions splitting the darkness in two.

Chapter Twenty-Five

<u>Meagan</u>

Chase pulled me down then threw himself over me, covering me, protecting me as always.

My mind was still reeling. Had he almost said what I'd prayed for him to say? I had seen it in his nervous eyes. Was there a chance?

Of course everything was ruined. Reality flashed back into my mind as I realized my brothers were in the camp under attack.

"Stay here," Chase hissed as he started to rise.

"NO!" I snapped as I pulled him back down. "You can't go. They won't know if you are a soldier or attacker."

He froze but was about to ignore me when there was a heavy WUMP, WUMP, WUMP sound. Repeated over and over, sometimes a burst of two, others of four. Once again, Chase threw himself over me, holding me down.

"The .50 Cals," he said as the machine gun continued to spray bullets into the night. The Army reaching out trying to touch someone with lethal force.

We lay there both unable to rise. I thought of my brothers and prayed they were smart enough to stay hidden. The Army would protect them. Right? I mean, what fools would attack a heavy machine gun? For what? The food had been offloaded. Why now?

Laying on the hard ground with Chase lying on top of me made my stomach tumble over itself. My heart raced. Not just from fear, but from a burning need deep inside my soul. A need for this man.

Eventually, the shooting stopped and still we lay there, neither wanting to move. Finally, Chase rolled off of me then called out. "It's us. Can we come in?"

There was a long silence then someone yelled back. "Yes, slow like."

When we got to the camp, I frantically searched for my brothers only to find them and Shaina hiding behind a log, half a dozen soldiers with rifles out protecting them. I sighed heavily then pulled them into the deepest hug.

"Where were you?" Austin demanded.

I glanced over at Chase and almost blushed. Nothing had happened. But what would people think? A young married couple sneaking off into the woods. Some of the smirks from the soldiers confirmed my worst fears. A combination of happiness for us and or jealousy.

We found the scowling lieutenant looking down at a wounded soldier being administered to.

"What happened?" Chase asked.

The lieutenant shook his head. "Some idiots attacked us. I guess they wanted what little food we had." He paused then shook his head again. "They won't be doing that again."

Chase nodded, "A machine gun can change a man's mind."

The Lieutenant sighed as he shone a flashlight off to the left. "So will being dead. Three of them. We'll bury them in the morning."

My heart broke. They looked so young. Only a few years older than Jimmy. Why? The wounds were ghastly. I thought of something like that happening to either of my brothers and wanted to throw up.

The Lieutenant cursed under his breath and said, "They're thinner than rails. I don't know their story. But if they'd have come in peaceful, we would have fed them."

I could see the anguish in his eyes. Three young boys lay dead. Something told me they would not be the last. People were getting desperate.

"Can I have one of their rifles?" Chase asked, pointing to a gun lying next to one of the boys.

The Lieutenant thought for a moment then nodded. "I've got men out searching. You can go through their pockets if they've got ammo, you can take it. One thing the army doesn't need is more guns."

Chase squatted down and started rifling through the boy's clothes. My stomach rebelled as I fought not to slap him. How could he be so cold? So unfeeling? It was almost sacrilege to be treating three young men like that. But I forced myself to keep quiet.

He looked up and caught me glaring at him. He didn't shoot me a guilty look but instead simply moved to the next boy and checked him.

When he finished, he held out a hand with six bullets. He then ejected six more from the rifle and nodded to himself. "Add 30, 30 shells to our list of things we need."

I scoffed as I turned away, suddenly realizing that once again everything had changed. Chase and I had had a moment. We were discussing important things. Feelings. But I knew in the depths of my soul that we wouldn't go back there.

Chase had been caught at a vulnerable moment. I'd trapped him and he'd seen my frustration. But what was I going to do about my feelings? Nothing. The attack had shown just how much I needed him. Not just today. But tomorrow, and on the road to his grandfather's.

And once we got there, I was going to need his approval to stay. My brother's very life depended upon Chase's continued protection. He held all the power in our situation.

I scrunched my eyes closed to stop from crying and took a deep breath. Just go with it, I told myself. Yes, I was using him. I realized it. But what more could I do? He didn't want me that way. To him, we, my brothers and I were simply people who needed protecting.

It had been that way ever since he'd stepped out of the forest. We weren't what he was searching for. We were simply a self-imposed obligation.

Laughing to myself, I turned away. The thing about it was, he wouldn't take what I was offering in payment. A sick feeling of rejection ate at my stomach. I owed him so much. I would do anything, literally anything he asked of me.

But he had to ask. I couldn't throw myself at him. I had already burdened him enough.

The next morning as we drove into Coeur d'Alene, I noticed that it was much like Boise.

People were already starting to get thin. Six weeks into things and it was getting bad. And this was a farm state. Idaho exported more food than it brought in.

But again, the people weren't where the food was. And I knew it was going to get so much worse. Fields were not being planted. People were living off what was left of last year's harvest.

People stopped to watch us pass then gathered as we pulled to a halt. I could see it in their eyes. Inspecting the empty wagons and feeling deprived. Cheated. We weren't bringing food.

More than one person glared at us with anger. Chase gave me a sad smile and I knew he was seeing what I was seeing. "At some point, they're going to head for the mountains. Cities are a death trap."

I nodded as I realized that even when we got to his grandfather's we wouldn't be completely safe.

The lieutenant held up his hand and pointed to where he wanted the wagons. Chase maneuvered the horses to the spot then handed over the reins to an army hostler who would take the horses.

Again, people silently stood and watched, waiting for some sign to give them hope.

Chase jumped down then reached up and grabbed me around the waist to lift me down. He held me in the air for a moment, looking up at me with tenderness. I swallowed hard and knew he could see the love in my eyes.

He put me down then broke my heart by turning away. Reaching over he patted the left wagon wheel horse on the neck and whispered something into his ear. He stood with his arms crossed and watched the horses being led away then sighed heavily. Turning to the Lieutenant he said, "Thank you for letting us tag along."

The Lieutenant glanced at me, and my brothers then shook his head. "It's a long walk up north. It won't be easy."

Chase shouldered his pack then grabbed his rifle from the back of the wagon. "I think you're going to have a harder time here in this city than we will on the road. I wouldn't want to be in your shoes a month from now. You're going to have to decide who eats and who doesn't. Who lives and who dies."

The Lieutenant nodded as he pursed his lips. "Don't think I haven't thought about that."

"Well, we'll hit the road. Thanks again."

"Hold on," he said as he swung down then grabbed a sack off the back of the last wagon. Tied off with string, it looked about three-quarters empty. My heart jumped in anticipation as he held it out for Chase. "Payment for driving the wagon. It freed up one of my soldiers."

Chase balked for a moment, unable to believe his luck. Then he quickly unshouldered his pack and stuffed the bag of wheat in, hiding it from prying eyes.

"Thank you, Lieutenant Carver," he said, holding out his hand.

The Lieutenant smiled for the first time since I had met him and said, "Maybe, if things get bad. I'll come find you up on that farm."

Chase laughed. "You'll be welcome. I think we will be needing men who can fight."

They clasped hands, shook, then both sighed, realizing that they would probably never meet again.

Chase nodded for us to go and pushed through the crowd of people who had circled the wagon. The glare of jealousy and hate in some of their eyes sent a nervous shudder down my spine. More than one stared with intense avarice at Chase's pack where he'd stored the bag of wheat.

He saw it too and grabbed my hand to hurry us away and to the relative safety of the road. It took almost an hour to work our way out of the city and onto the road headed north. It was only when I felt a sense of safety that I realized he was still holding my hand.

My heart jumped. If you had told me six weeks earlier that a boy like Chase Conrad would hold my hand. Nope, no way.

Glancing over I noticed a scowl as if he was angry. My heart fell as I started to pull my hand back, but he clasped it harder and said, "We need to talk."

My heart raced as my mind immediately jumped back to the other night before we were attacked.

"About?" I managed to say.

He sighed heavily. "About how I should introduce you when we get to my Papa's."

I felt my brow furrow as I stared at him trying to figure out what he was fighting to say.

He saw my confusion then said, "We don't have to pretend anymore. We're away from the army. In the middle of Idaho. Nobody is going to try and make you leave the state."

My heart fell. It was over. I just knew it.

He sighed heavily. "If you want, we can just annul the marriage ourselves. We don't need anything official. No one around here knows except for your brothers. We … We haven't done anything. So. We can just pretend it never happened."

Without thinking I started to twist my grandmother's ring and fought to keep the tears from spilling down my face. "Is that what you want?" I managed to say as I held my breath.

"What I want isn't important," he growled. "What do you want? What is best for you?"

My tears flashed over to instant anger. "No," I snapped. "You are always doing that. Putting everyone else's needs ahead of yours. I will not let you ruin your life. Tie you to a promise you made just to save us. No."

His forehead crinkled into a dozen frown lines as he stared off into the distance.

My heart broke into a thousand pieces. "I won't lie to your family. I can't live off their kindness while lying to them."

Without turning away from staring at the far mountains he said, "You wouldn't ruin my life."

I slammed to a halt and turned him to face me. "What do you mean? Exactly." My heart was racing, my lungs had forgotten how to work, and my entire world stopped spinning while I waited for an answer that might change my life forever.

"I said, you wouldn't ruin my life."

"What does that mean," I asked. I need to hear the words. I needed to know it was real.

He shrugged then turned to stare into my eyes. "It means exactly what I said. Being married to you. For reals, would not ruin my life..."

I scoffed and started to pull away, a less romantic statement had never been spoken in the history of the English language.

"No," he said, holding me back. "You didn't let me finish. It wouldn't ruin my life. In fact, it would make my life worth living."

I frowned at him as I tried to understand. No way this was possible.

He let out a long breath then said, "Miss Meagan Foster. Will you marry me? Will you allow me to proclaim to the world that I love you and only you? That I've loved you since the first time I saw you. Let me tell the world how much I admire your strength and courage. How I am driven crazy by the wiggle in your walk and the fire in your eyes. How I hope to fall asleep next to you every night for the rest of my life and always wake up with you in my arms."

My jaw dropped open as I forced myself to breathe. Was this Chase Conrad saying these words?

He smiled then said, "I'd get down on one knee, but I'd never get back up with this pack on my back."

"Do you mean it?" I asked as my mind fought to believe what I was hearing.

He smiled, then scoffed. "Do you really think I would say those words if I didn't mean them? I sound like a Hallmark movie."

I stared up into his eyes and saw the truth, Without thinking, I threw myself at him, my arms wrapping around his neck so I could pull him down and kiss him like a woman kisses her man.

After half of forever, we broke apart to catch our breath, our foreheads resting against each other's.

Austin coughed. Both boys had kept going and waited about a hundred feet up the road. Obviously giving us privacy. I felt my face flush with heat, I had basically attacked Chase and my brothers had stood there and watched.

Chase smiled then said, "Just so you know. You'll be sleeping under the tarp with me tonight. The boys and Shaina can have the tent."

My heart soared. Yes, he was being dictatorial, but I wasn't going to complain. Not when I was getting everything I had ever hoped for. Life was so perfect. At least at that exact moment. Of course, it wouldn't stay that way. We couldn't be that lucky. There would be no happy ever after.

Chapter Twenty-Seven

<u>Chase</u>

I woke up the next morning with Meagan in my arms. Lifting up, I saw she was awake with a smile a mile wide staring up at me. Believe me, there is no better way to greet the day.

"Morning gorgeous," I said.

She hugged me and laid her head on my chest. "Can we just stay here for the rest of our lives?"

Laughing, I pushed up. "I wish. But the boys are going to get hungry in the next day or two."

Pouting, she joined me as we woke the boys. James shot me a frown then pulled me aside.

"You and Meagan. I thought it was supposed to be pretend."

I stared down at him then smiled. "We love each other."

His frown deepened. "If you hurt her. I will kill you in your sleep."

The venom in his voice let me know he was not joking around. A lot of things had changed over the last few weeks. But a brother's protective instincts were not one of them.

"I understand," I said as I gave him my best serious look.

He sighed then asked Meagan what was for breakfast.

She had Austin grind some wheat which she used to make flat pancakes or fluffy tortillas. The wheat the lieutenant had given us would make all the difference. We should be at my Papa's in two days.

Tim had said both Ryan and Haley were ahead of us. Had they arrived safely? My heart soared at the thought of introducing them to Meagan. My wife. Really, it didn't get better than that.

We had walked most of the day along the edge of the mountains. Trees on both sides of the road. A sharp pine aroma hung in the air with a hint of cedar and moldy needles.

It was almost evening, and I was thinking about the night before us when I felt the first shiver down my spine. Shaina felt it too as she constantly checked over her shoulder. Meagan held my hand and was babbling about her friends in high school and how they would be jealous then she remembered that Reno had burned to the ground and started off on how terrible that was.

I ignored her as I dropped her hand and unshouldered my rifle.

"What?" she asked.

273

"Get the boys behind cover," I told her as I pointed to the trees at the top of a small hill.

"Why?"

"I think we are being followed," I told her as I motioned for her to hurry the boys into the trees. Once they were under cover, I pulled my binoculars from my pack and started examining our back trail.

Why? I wondered. What had set off my alarms? And Shaina's, I reminded myself. That dog didn't spook easily. I wasn't being stupid. She had felt it also.

Sitting on the pine needles, my arms resting on my knees, I slowly scanned back down the road, then off to the sides. It took me ten minutes to spot them. Two men flitting from tree to tree. Mid-twenties, both armed with rifles.

The smart thing would be to just shoot them now. I knew I could get one at least before the other disappeared. But a big chunk of civilization remained inside of me. The part that said you can't shoot someone just because they were behind you.

But why were they hiding? Really, the only reason was to approach us unseen. Why? Because we had what they wanted. What did men want? Food, and a woman. It really was that simple, I thought as an anger began to build inside of me. NO, this was not happening.

"Here," I said as I handed the rifle to Meagan. This was going to require close in work. The pistol would be better.

Her face drained of color as she looked down at the rifle then at me.

"Keep the boys here, stay off the road. No fire. Keep Shaina on her leash."

"But ... but, why? No, you can't."

Ignoring her, I broke into the trees so I could work my way around to where I wanted to meet these two. Really it was the only way. If I pretended they weren't there. If I ignored them they'd take us in the night. Or along the road when we least expected.

No, the only solution was to stop them now. Crouching low, I worked my way down the backside of the ridge then crossed back over to come in behind them. As I wormed my way down the hill I thought about Meagan and all I could lose.

For the first time since my mom had died, I felt fear. Fear of losing what I might have had with Meagan. The thought of not having that life made me shiver inside. Several things happened at once. For one, I realized I had made the right decision about telling her how I felt. Two, that I was the luckiest man in the history of men. And three, I could not screw this up.

275

She and the boys were depending upon me.

I came down off the hill and crossed the road to the same side I'd seen our pursuers. Hurrying from tree to tree I found their trail. Scuff marks in the pine needles, a bent willow shoot, and smiled to myself. These were not woodsmen. Something that might be important. Tim or Ryan would never have left this big a trail.

But these two didn't think anyone would be tracking them. They were the hunter, not the hunted. Surprise would be my ally.

I spotted them at the bottom of the hill looking up to where we'd stepped off the road, wondering where we'd disappeared to. Both dressed in jeans and flannel shirts. The youngest, maybe twenty, had long hair in a mullet. The oldest by a few years had a crew cut. They both looked at each other, silently asking what they should do.

This was why I hadn't brought Shaina. A bark now and I would be discovered. Instead, I ducked behind a tree. Every time their focus was forward I would flit to the next tree. Always drawing closer. Finally, I got to within one tree of Mr. Mullet. The younger guy.

Now or never, I told myself as I stepped out and put my gun against his head. "Freeze," I yelled. "Or he dies."

I will be honest with you. I expected the other guy to freeze. I was in control, I could shoot this man any time I wanted. Nothing could stop me. His friend would freeze and wait to hear my terms.

One of the most wrong things I have ever assumed. The guy swung his rifle towards us. I stared, unable to believe the hate in his eyes as he pulled the trigger. The bullet ripped through his friend and then into me. It was like a hot poker had been shoved through my side.

A numbness hit me. Really, disbelief. This wasn't supposed to go this way.

Mullet man was leaning against the tree looking down at the blood oozing out from the wound in his side with pure shock. Either at being wounded or the treachery of his friend. Crew cut guy was jacking in another round.

I did what any sane man would do and jumped behind the tree Mr. Mullet was using and fired. A snapshot that caught Mr. Crew Cut square in the chest as he tried to jack another round into the breech. I will never forget the look of shock in his eyes as he stared down at his brand new sucking chest wound, red bubbles of blood appearing on his shirt pocket.

He looked up at me with a confused frown, then dropped dead.

I didn't mourn. Really, I couldn't care less. The man was no longer a threat. Besides, my side was killing me.

"His brother will kill you," Mr. Mullet said as he pressed onto his side, frantically trying to stop the bleeding.

I shoved my pistol into my belt, grabbed the man's rifle then the one off the dead guy, and started up the hill. He wasn't going to be able to hurt us. The wound in my side burned with each step. Meagan, I thought to myself I had to get to Meagan.

She squealed when she saw me and ran towards me, ready to throw herself at me when she saw the blood seeping out from between my fingers. "No," she screamed. Then immediately fell into mom mode, telling Austin to start a fire and for Jimmy to cut a shirt for bandages.

"What happened," she said as she led me to the shade and helped me sit down.

"I was shot."

She rolled her eyes at me but focused on pulling my hand away so she could see how bad it was. "Here," she demanded as she made me lay down on a blanket then proceeded to cut away my shirt.

"Hey," I mumbled. "Those are expensive."

She laughed then took a deep breath as she forced herself to do what was necessary. After a few minutes, she let out a long sigh. "It went through you."

"That means two wounds."

She smiled sadly, "It means I don't have to dig around looking for the bullet."

I sort of checked out after that and let her do her thing. But my soul soared with pride. My woman didn't fall apart at the first sign of trouble. She took charge and cared for me with tenderness but firm assurance. Just what a man needed in this new world.

She ended up wrapping me in bandages then sat back, wiping the hair out of her eyes with a bloody hand, leaving a red streak across her forehead. "I don't think it got any of the intestines. An inch more and I wouldn't be able to fix you."

I nodded, repressing a shudder at the thought of being gut-shot.

"What happened?" she asked. Both boys stood behind her, desperate to hear.

So, I explained, the whole getting the drop on the guy and getting shot anyway. "I guess they weren't friends after all."

Jimmy frowned then said, "I want one of the rifles."

I laughed then nodded. "Meagan can have the other."

"Hey," Austin said, obviously put out.

"You've got Shaina."

Meagan sighed then told them to set up camp. We had enough water we would just stay there for the night. She had them set up the tarp between three threes then helped me up and over to it.

Every instinct was to move us along. We were a target here. That man, the wounded one, had mentioned the dead guy's brother. Had Mr. Mullet made it back? Was he still alive? Did we need to worry?

But a wave of tiredness washed through me. I wasn't moving. Not tonight, I realized.

As I was lying down, I shot Meagan a quick glance and shook my head. "This was not how I was planning on spending tonight."

She blushed beautifully then said, "We have our whole lives. Skipping a night or two won't kill you."

"Who said anything about two nights? One, if I have to. But no more."

Again she blushed but I could tell she was happy to know I wanted her that much.

The next morning I had them bring over my pack and started seeing what I could get rid of. Some I unloaded onto the boys' backpacks. But we were going to be at my papa's in two days. I got the pack down to about thirty pounds then pushed myself up.

Meagan hurried to help me, but I shook her off. If I couldn't stand on my own, then I wasn't going to be able to walk to my grandfathers.

We had put two miles behind us when I had to stop and rest. The gunshot had taken the last of my reserves. Meagan glanced over at me from beneath her brow not wanting me to see the concern in her eyes.

I shot her a quick wink then pushed myself up. "Slow but steady," I said.

She hurried over and slipped an arm around my waist. "Let us carry the stuff in your pack."

I scoffed and then focused on putting one foot in front of the other. I was lucky, The wound didn't hurt too much, and the bleeding had stopped yesterday. It would hurt like hell when Meagan tried to change the bandages. But that was days away if I had a vote.

No, I could do this.

She hovered, ready to help me. I could see it in her eyes. Pure terror. It tore me apart thinking how much she would be hurt if anything happened to me. She and the boys would be all alone. "Meagan," I said. "If anything happens to me. You go to my grandfather. Tell him you are my widow ..."

"Chase," she gasped.

"... my widow," I repeated. "He will take you in. You and the boys. It's about ten miles up the road. A big boulder on the right side guarding the dirt road to his house."

"Chase," she cried as she shook her head. "Are you hurting? The wound ..."

"No," I assured her. "just in case."

Rolling her eyes at me she reached over and took my hand. "Shut up. Do not talk about stuff like that."

"Meagan ..."

"NO." She growled. "Don't you dare." She squeezed my hand fiercely, demanding I do as she commanded.

Sighing, I nodded. This wasn't a fight I was going to win.

We continued on in silence, both lost in our own world or what might be, but still holding hands.

That evening I had the boys stop by a creek where Ryan, Tim, and I had camped on numerous times. After showing the boys where they could fish, I crashed under the tarp and only woke when Meagan poked at me, demanding I get up so I could eat.

Glaring at her I forced my eyes open. She was right, I needed the fuel, but that didn't mean I was going to forgive her anytime soon.

I had just finished the last of the fish when I sighed heavily and once more crawled in under the tarp. I knew Meagan would join me later, but I just couldn't keep my eyes open and wait for her.

Instead, I fell asleep thinking about a man with a rifle, a man who knew how to use one.

Chapter Twenty-Eight

<u>Meagan</u>

My heart was breaking. A sense of hopelessness filled my entire being. I was going to lose him. I just knew it. I could see it in the way he moved. Slowly, not the confident walk of Chase Conrad. He was in pain. He was flushed. Obviously, an infection was setting in. But it was in the eyes that he exposed himself. They kept glazing over. Like he was already checking out.

"Here," I said as I moved up next to him and slipped my arm into his.

He glanced down at me, his eyes held a confused veneer, then he recognized me and gave me a quick smile.

Please, I begged. Please help him. We should stop. He should be in a hospital. I should be able to call EMTs. The police. There should be someone to help us. But we were alone.

Later that morning we passed a farmhouse off to the left. I asked Chase if we should stop.

He frowned for a moment, obviously confused about what I was talking about but then came back to reality and shook his head. "They're jerks," he said. "I wouldn't trust them. Papa's only about three miles up the road."

My heart jumped we were so close. They would know what to do. Would they have medicines? His grandfather had owned a farm, surely he knew how to take care of an injury. Maybe he could sew up Chase's wounds.

Both Austin and Jimmy kept shooting me concerned looks. They could see it just like me. Chase wasn't all there.

That's probably why we were so easy to attack. If Chase had been totally aware they never would have gotten so close. We were just cresting a small hill when a shot rang out and I felt the buzz of a passing bullet.

Chase knocked me to the ground with his shoulder then turned, lifting his rifle, he fired three times downhill then motioned for me to take the boys and get off the ridge. Standing there like a wall while shots continued from down the hill until we were out of the field of fire.

"Go," he said pointing to the forest.

Two more shots rang out as we ducked between trees. My heart raced. Someone was trying to kill us. Were the friends of the man Chase had killed? It didn't matter, I realized as I pushed Austin to keep going. The farther away we could go the better.

Suddenly Shaina barked and tugged at her leash, but to our left, not behind us.

"This way," Chase yelled as he shifted our route to the right.

We continued to race through the trees until we suddenly came to a cliff face. A cliff we could never climb.

"Damn," Chase mumbled under his breath. "I forgot about this." He frowned as he looked up at the cliff then in each direction, his hand resting on the cliff face while he caught his breath. "Here," he said as he pointed north.

We followed him. Twice more shots pierced the afternoon. My heart pounded in my chest. It wasn't fair. We were so close. Chase had done so much to get us here and it was all going to be taken away from us.

The beautiful life I was going to have with the man I loved. I was going to lose it. An anger filled me as I turned and fired three shots from my rifle. I had no target. I just had to do something. They were trying to kill my man.

The pain in my shoulder surprised me. The ringing in my ears I should have expected. But it was the stink of gunpowder that shocked me. I'd just tried to kill someone.

Chase gently pushed my rifle down then pointed to a set of boulders. We were rushing towards them when he collapsed, grabbing his leg just as another shot echoed off the cliff face.

"NO," I screamed as I saw him grab his thigh. Once again, he had been shot. The bubbling blood leaking out from between his fingers.

My stomach clenched in pure fear. Men behind us were getting closer. Chase was wounded, twice.

"Jimmy, Austin," he growled, "Get me to the rocks."

Both boys looked back at him with wide eyes, unable to understand what he needed.

"Grab my collar and pull me," he said through gritted teeth. "Meagan, keep guard, shoot anything you see move."

I was torn between guarding and going to him.

As the boys pulled him towards the boulder, he used his good leg to help them along. I moved behind them, covering the approaches to the boulders. An ancient rockslide had carved out a chunk from the forest, giving me a clean field of fire. Rocks the size of cars sat at the bottom of the cliff. I could see a hundred yards in any direction.

When I moved into the pile of large boulders, I saw Chase tying his backpack's drawstring around his upper thigh and pulling it tight. He slipped a stick into the string then twisted it, creating a tourniquet before tying it off.

Both of the boys were looking at him, then me, obviously wanting us to solve this problem. Chase was wounded, again. Men were trying to kill us. This was not what little boys should be experiencing.

I turned to look back into the forest, terrified at what I would find. How many were there? Who were they? Could I shoot someone?

Yes, I realized. Six weeks ago. Before the impact. Never in a thousand years. Memories of my mother would have stopped me. But now. I had been hardened, I'd endured too much to let someone take it away from me. My brothers, Chase, their lives depended upon me doing what needed to be done.

"Here," Chase said as he asked for the boys to help him up. He hobbled over to a large boulder to look over the rim down the slope into the forest.

Suddenly two shots ricocheted off the rocks behind us. Chase flinched, dropping down then reached up and pulled me down next to him.

I could feel his heart pounding in his chest. When I looked into his eyes I saw a worry. Not fear, but a worry. It was us, I realized, me and the boys. He was desperate to protect us. Glancing left and right I could see his mind trying to work out a solution.

We were trapped. They would get us. Either stand off and wait until we died of thirst or move in when we were too weak to fight.

"Austin," Chase said as his forehead frowned. "I need you to take Shaina behind that rock over there. Get into that crevice. Put my backpack in the opening. Your job is to keep Shaina alive."

Austin frowned back at him. "Ricochets'," Chase said. "We're going to need Shaina."

I instantly understood. He was giving Austin a reason to do what was best for him. Getting him out of the line of fire. Chase then turned to me and rolled his eyes. "I'd tell you to join him, but you wouldn't listen to me."

Scoffing, I half crouched to peek over the boulder just to make sure we weren't being charged.

"What about me," Jimmy asked as he lifted his rifle.

"Give me that," Chase said as he held out his hand.

"What, No," Jimmy gasped.

Chase shook his head. "You're not going to need it where you're going."

Jimmy frowned as my stomach turned over.

Letting out a long breath, Chase pointed north, along the face of the cliff, "I need you to get to my grandfather. Tell him we're trapped, to bring his gun. He'll know what to do."

"No," I snapped.

Chase's head dropped to his chest. "We don't have a choice. I can't get you lot there. Not now." He glared down at his wounded leg with a fierce anger.

"But …"

"Stop," Jimmy demanded. "Just stop Meagan. He's right. It is our best chance."

I fought to understand. My brother was eleven years old. This was too much danger. Too much responsibility.

Ignoring me, Chase leaned over to draw in the sand. "We're here," he said as he drew an X next to a long line. "Here is the cliff face. And this is the road. Work your way along the cliff face, darting from boulder to boulder until you can get into the forest. Then once you're clear. Work over to the road.

Jimmy nodded.

"Two miles up, on the right you will see a big boulder. As big as these. Follow that dirt road until you come to a farm. You can't go any further."

He nodded.

"Leave your pack, everything. You run like the wind. You understand."

"Yes, Sir," Jimmy said as he took a deep breath.

"You can do this," Chase told him. "When you get to the end of these boulders. You look back and wave. Meagan and I will cover you, keeping their heads down."

Jimmy swallowed hard then he shot me a half smile. I could see the fear in his eyes but there was also a determination that I knew I would never defeat. He was set on a mission. A man's mission and he would refuse to back down.

Without thinking, I reached out and pulled him into a hug. "You be careful."

He pulled away from me, obviously not wanting the dreaded sister's hug. He gave me a quick smile. Poked Austin in the foot in his crevice then scurried along the cliff face, darting from rock to rock.

When he was in position he waved. I helped Chase up. We both fired three shots each, taking turns. I glanced over and saw Jimmy jumping over a log and into the forest. There was one long shot from our left but my brother made it into the cover of the trees.

I was about to fire again when Chase put a hand on my arm and pulled me down. "We need to save ammunition. From here on, only if you've got a clear target."

I nodded as I looked up the line and saw that Jimmy had disappeared. Would I ever see him again? What if he was hurt or captured? A thousand fears danced in my stomach. Please, I begged. Please keep him safe.

I turned to find Chase with his head down, fighting to stay together. Beads of sweat dripped down his face. A pale clammy tone to his skin made my stomachache.

Chase pulled himself up and hobbled over behind another boulder, something that would give him better cover. Using his binoculars he scanned the forest, suddenly he dropped them to hang on the strap around his neck and pulled his rifle up for a quick shot.

A scream from the forest told me he'd hit someone. My heart soared. We weren't helpless. I started to stand up, but he pushed me back down. "Not yet," he told me. "When I tell you, over there, behind that rock, but use Jimmy's rifle."

I frowned at him.

He laughed, "I want them to think there are three of us. Not Two. Different calibers sound different. It might slow them down."

Nodding, I crawled to where he pointed then waited for him to give me the sign.

"One shot, Next to that big cedar on your right."

I took a deep breath then stood, fired one shot then dropped back down.

"Did I hit anything?" I asked him breathlessly.

He shrugged. "You scared them. That is what we needed."

Suddenly a dozen shots erupted from the forest. The bullets bounced off the cliff behind us. Chase winced as he ducked down holding his right shoulder.

I cursed under my breath as I hurried to his side. But it wasn't too bad, just a ragged flesh wound. I almost laughed as I fought to stop from giggling. This was so stupid, but I couldn't help myself. A month prior, I'd have freaked out at such a wound. But this was nothing compared to holes in his side and another in his thigh. Believe me, we had bigger problems.

I crawled over to my backpack and pulled out a T-shirt then grabbed his knife off his belt and cut it into strips. I tied two of them around his thigh wound and another around his upper arm.

"You're getting to have more holes than a pin cushion," I said as I tied off the last bandage.

He smiled then leaned forward and kissed me. "I love you," he whispered. "More than you will ever know."

My heart melted. God, he was so perfect. He knew what I needed. He always knew.

Leaning forward I rested my forehead against his. "Please stop getting shot. A girl wants a guy without so many holes. Okay?"

He laughed then we both heard something, a yelp and the snap of a branch. Chase put a hand on my shoulder to steady him as he rose then cursed as he snapped a quick shot.

A big man in a red flannel shirt was trying to get close to us but fell back into the trees.

"How long can we survive?" I asked him. "I mean before they get to us."

He shrugged. "Listen. When I give you the word. You and Austin head out. Follow James's path. They want me."

My jaw dropped as I stared at him, "Don't be stupid. I am not leaving you. Besides, they've moved to cover that part."

"I'm not leaving either," Austin called from his hole.

Chase's head dropped as he took a deep breath then checked his rifle, then mine, and finally Jimmy's. He then pulled his pistol and put it on a rock next to the rock he was hiding behind. "Sixteen bullets." He said with a shake of his head. "That is all we have left."

My stomach clenched as I saw the fear in his eyes. He knew we weren't going to make it. That we would never be able to keep them away with only sixteen bullets.

Chapter Twenty-Nine

Chase

My head pounded as I tried to focus. How had we gotten into this crap? I was almost home. Almost safe then it all went south. I ached in a dozen different places. My head spun like it was on a circus ride and the love of my life was in danger.

Taking a deep breath I tried to think. Tried to figure a way out. I'd sent James but I figured that was maybe a thirty percent chance of working. Either they'd get him along the way, or he'd get lost, or Papa wouldn't believe him. Probably closer to a twenty percent chance of working.

And even then. What could one old man do? Yes, I knew it was my grandfather. The man had been awarded a Silver Star for what he did in Vietnam. But that was Fifty years ago.

Reaching up, I pulled myself up to peek over the edge of the boulder. Who were these guys? There had to be at least four of them. I think I'd winged one. So three and a half were out there.

We weren't going to make it, I realized. Everything told me we were just outgunned. Trapped. I couldn't get them out of here. Meagan and Austin. When James raced across the opening to the forest someone had moved into that position and blocked our way out.

Sixteen bullets. It would have been seventeen, but I'd traded that one for three shirts. Believe me, I was second-guessing that decision hard.

As I peered over the edge of my boulder I saw a quick movement off to the left. Someone in blue flitting to the next tree. I held my fire, the figure was too fast, there a moment then gone. Grinding my teeth I forced my finger away from the trigger.

I glanced over at Meagan and felt my heart break. If I gave up, would they let her and Austin go? If I thought they would then I'd do it in a heartbeat. But I knew deep in my soul that they'd never let her go.

She was too pretty. Too pure and in this new world too valuable. They would use her then throw her to the side when there was nothing left to take.

My gut clenched as an anger filled me. I'd kill them all before I let that happen. But a doubt ate around the edges. If they got me, killed me, then Meagan would be lost to them.

Studying her for a quiet moment I felt my heart swell. My wife. My responsibility. My reason for living. So beautiful. And she loved me. ME! Looking up she caught me staring at her and smiled. The confidence in her eyes hit me in the gut. She expected me to save them. She knew I would save them.

Suddenly there were three shots from the forest. I twisted away but not before I saw the man in blue dart out of the trees to a large boulder. Before I could shoot, he was gone.

They were getting closer. These were not idiots. They worked as a team. Someone was in charge. My gut told me it was the guy in blue. He was using the others to draw our attention so he could work in closer.

I limped over to Meagan's boulder and rested my rifle on top, looking down the barrel towards the trees. If they were smart, they'd try to get a second guy closer. That meant we would be fired at, and someone would race forward.

Holding my breath I waited. He would come from behind that big cedar. I just knew it. The question was, would it be from the left side or the right? The right I guessed.

Placing my finger on the trigger I waited.

Suddenly the air exploded as a half dozen shots erupted, the bullets pinging off the cliff face behind us.

I held steady and didn't duck down. There, on the right side like I predicted our man in red flannel. I fired, he spun then dropped face first and stopped moving. The man I had wounded earlier, I realized. I took careful aim and put another bullet into him.

There were three attackers left.

More shots rang out forcing me to duck. A shot ricocheted into my backpack protecting Austin knocking it to the side. The boy looked through the new opening with wide eyes, hugging Shaina's neck, terrified. But he smiled at me and pulled the pack back into place.

I groaned when I saw chilly oozing out of the hole. I'd been saving that last can. The thought of losing food was just so wrong, but then I laughed when I realized starving to death was the least of our problems. Oh, I hoped we lived so long.

Closing my eyes, I tried to gather strength. Taking a deep breath I glanced over to find Meagan standing behind her rock looking down range. God, what a woman. Fighting next to me. Most people would have been a quivering mess. Not my Meagan.

The pride I felt was almost overwhelming and I swear a tear did not form in the corner of my eye. But the woman was just too good. And I was going to lose her. I just knew it.

Suddenly she fired then cursed, shooting me an apologetic glance. "I thought I had him, but he moved just as I shot."

I nodded as I dragged myself over next to her. If we were going to die, we were going to do it together. Lifting up, I joined her in scanning our front. There were three of them. Some unknown off to the left. Blue shirt guy in the middle. And camouflage guy off to the right who had moved in to block James's escape path.

"Why?" Meagan asked. "It can't be worth dying over."

I shrugged as a man in green flitted to another tree off to our left. I threw a quick shot but missed. They were wearing us down, making me use ammunition. Twelve, I told myself, and six of those were for the pistol.

My heart broke that I'd brought Meagan and the boys into this hell. It wasn't right. We should have stayed in the camps. We were fed, it was safe. But no, I had to go home, and as a result. The people I loved were in danger.

Pure anger filled me as I ground my back teeth, praying for a chance to kill again. I'd killed two men in the last two days and felt no remorse, not even a twinge. I'd do it again in a heartbeat if it meant my people got to live.

Suddenly the blue shirt guy jumped behind the next rock, ten feet closer.

Sighing, I closed my eyes and fought against the pain pumping through me. The hot sun reflected off the cliff face burning the back of my neck.

How long would it take James to get there? Too long, I realized. We'd never last long enough.

Suddenly Meagan fired at Camouflage guy then cursed under her breath when she missed. She then held out her hand for James's rifle as she was out of ammunition.

My gut tightened as I handed it over. Five rifle shots left.

That was how we spent the rest of the morning. Them flitting between cover, us taking a shot.

Four.

A ricochet snipping Meagan's calf. Me being pissed and shooting back.

Three.

Two.

Meagan squinted then pointed at a foot exposed from behind a rock. I smiled at her and took careful aim. I had the perfect shot and fired.

The man screamed and pulled his foot back.

One. Then it would be the pistol only.

My gut squeezed. Once they knew we were out of rifle ammo they'd move in even closer. And if they then waited until dark, they would have us. No problem.

Suddenly they started firing. We ducked down but my heart broke when my pistol resting on a rock for quick action suddenly flew into the air. I could only stare in disbelief as I saw it disintegrate. A round had caught it directly in the action and rendered it useless.

Meagan's eyes grew with disbelief as she stared at the now useless gun then at me.

God, I had been such an idiot. I'd left the gun out where I could get it. I'd been worried about my leg going out from under me and landing on my right side, trapping the gun on my hip, rendering it useless.

But this was worse.

"I'm sorry," I whispered to her.

She gave me a soft smile then leaned over and whispered, "I love you."

I could see it in her eyes. She knew this was the end. They would kill me, then take her. I will be honest, I wondered about using the last bullet on her.

She looked into my eyes, and I knew she knew what I was thinking. My insides rebelled but I didn't dismiss the idea until she reached over and took my knife from its sheath. "We'll go down fighting, together."

My heart swelled with pure pride as I nodded then lifted up. I was going to get the guy in the blue shirt. He was the leader. I had one shot.

"Stay here," I hissed at Meagan then hobbled over to the next boulder then the next. Once in place I dropped down and crawled forward. Maybe if I could get into position, I could get this guy. Maybe the other two would stop. They didn't know how many bullets I had left.

I worked my way into a position, If I could get him to come out, I could kill him. He didn't know I was here, at this angle.

Tossing a rock off to the side I quickly lined up my shot and waited but he didn't bite. I was about to throw another stone when a shot showered me in gravel. Twisting I saw camouflage guy lining up for a second shot. While I'd been crawling forward, he'd been crawling in from the left.

I really had no choice, I fired my last shot and watched it strike at the shoulder slash neck crux, and plow into his insides. He flopped over and stared up into the sky with sightless eyes.

My insides rejoiced I'd eliminated another enemy, but I was out of ammunition. My heart sank as I realized I had failed. Meagan would be taken. I had led her here, to this fate. Everything was my fault.

Gritting my teeth, I stood and raised my rifle like a club as I hobbled forward, determined to finish this.

"Chase," Meagan called from behind me.

I ignored her. There would be no long goodbye. No final kiss. I was going to die trying to kill this man. But there was no other choice.

Suddenly, Blue shirt guy stood up from behind his boulder and scoffed to himself. "You killed my brother," he cursed as he put his rifle to his shoulder and took aim at my chest.

I dragged my leg behind me as I took another step towards him when the quiet of the day was broken by the crack of a rifle. Flinching, I twisted, expecting to be blown into oblivion. There was no pain. No shock.

Had he missed? My brow furrowed as I looked up to find blue-shirt guy staring at me in shock, a rather large round hole in his chest pumping blood.

Freezing I tried to understand. How. Twisting I looked over my shoulder. "Meagan?" I asked.

"Not me," She said as she pointed to the forest.

Two men were stepping out from the trees. One of the biggest guys I had seen and

Ryan. My cousin. Between them, James pointing towards us.

He'd made it. The boy had saved us. I didn't know how, all I knew was that my Meagan would live. That was all that was important.

Collapsing I suddenly felt her holding me, pushing the hair out of my eyes as she examined my wounds then smiled softly down at me. "You will not die. Not today."

I smiled up at her. "Never. We have a life to live. Children to raise, and a future to build."

Her smile grew as a tear raced down her cheek. "I will always love you."

Good, I thought as I let the darkness take me. My woman would care for me. I could finally relax. We had made it.

Epilogue

Chase

It was the smell of soap that pulled me up out of the darkness. I cracked an eye open to realize I was lying in a soft bed and Meagan was sitting there, waiting for me to return.

"Morning Princess," I croaked through dry lips.

She smiled widely and held a glass of water to my lips. "I knew you would come back. I never doubted it."

Smiling, I took her hand then fell back onto the bed. "My grandfather?"

Her smile faded as she shook her head. "He was killed. Squatters. Ryan killed them and took this place back. Your sister is here with her boyfriend, or I guess fiancé."

"Not unless I approve," I growled.

She laughed. "You're sister is too much like you. You will never control her."

I sighed, just letting myself rest, catching my breath when the door opened, and the room was flooded. James and Austin both smiled hesitantly.

"You two did good. I couldn't have been prouder."

Both boys swelled with pride.

Then I saw my sister, she was holding the hand of the small giant, the guy I had seen with Ryan stepping out of the forest. And a baby with the other hand. I glanced at their hands and then up at her as she stared up at him and realized nothing could stop those two from getting together.

Then I saw Ryan and a pretty brunette. "Thanks, man,"

He smiled, "You made it easy. Kept his attention long enough."

I sighed then glanced around the room. It was filled with people I didn't know. Two older women, a bunch of kids. A sadness filled me at the thought of losing Papa. I had wanted him to meet Meagan. He would have approved then punched me in the shoulder and told me I didn't deserve her.

He would have been right.

"How are we set up," I asked Ryan.

He smiled then shook his head. "That is so you. You think you're in charge."

I laughed. "We will work out the details later. Any sign of Cassie?"

Ryan shook his head with a sad expression. "Nothing. I'm thinking about going south to find her."

"Not before I'm healed up enough to go with you."

He laughed, "We'll work out the details later."

I sighed heavily then slumped back onto the bed. Meagan saw my weakness and hurried everyone out of the room before returning to me.

"Your family is so nice," she said. "And they have food. Enough to last until the harvest is in." She hesitated for a moment then added, "I told them we were married. They believed me."

I could only nod as I fought to stay awake. My family, my tribe, I realized. We would have to endure endless hardships. But we would do it together. Helping each other to rebuild our world.

And I got to do it with this beautiful girl. As if reading my mind she leaned forward to kiss me on the forehead. "I want children. So you get better quick."

I looked up into her eyes and felt my world fall into place. She would raise a nation of warriors, I realized. A man couldn't ask for more.

THE END

Author's Afterword

I do hope you enjoyed the novel. My last series explored what happens when everyone dies, and technology is lost. This time, I wanted to explore what happens when Technology is lost resulting in everyone dying. Again, the important question, what would I do in that situation.

I have often wondered what would happen if my family was separated by great distance when the world ended?

As always, I wish to thank friends who have helped, authors Erin Scott, and Anya Monroe. And my special friend Sheryl Turner. But most of all I want to thank my wife Shelley for all she puts up with. It can be difficult being an author's spouse. We have a tendency to live in our own little worlds. Our minds drifting to strange new places, keeping us unaware of what is happening around us. Thankfully I am married to a woman who knows when to let me write and knows when to pull me back into the real world.

The first book in the series Impact (The End of Times 1) is available on Amazon. I hope to have the next book in the series, "Survivors", out in a few months. In the mean time, I have put in a small sample of the first book in my other series, The End of Everything (The End of Everything 1) truly believe you would enjoy it.

Thank you again.

Nate Johnson

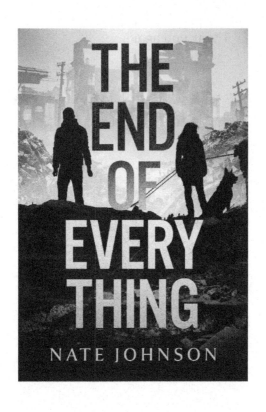

The End of Everything

Chapter One

Nick

I didn't say goodbye to my mom that day. A fact that I would regret on my deathbed. Being an angry seventeen-year-old was my only excuse. It was my mom who sent me away. Her way of stopping me from becoming an even worse jerk.

A boy gets in one fight and the world comes crashing down on him. Granted, breaking a guy's arm and knocking out a couple of teeth for the other one made it seem worse. But then they had it coming, believe me.

Anyway, Mom figured six weeks as a Counselor in Training at Camp Tecumseh in Eastern Pennsylvania would keep me away from bad influences. A nice peaceful summer, she said. God, how wrong could a person be?

But like I said, I didn't even turn to look at her when I stepped up onto the bus. If I'd known I'd never see her again, I might have given a damn. I might not have been such a jerk. At least I like to think so. It's how I keep from beating myself up about it.

I nodded to the driver. The same guy I remembered from my camp five years earlier. Then Dad died and going away to summer camp became an unnecessary expense. But Mom thought it would be good for me to do this CIT thing. It didn't cost anything. Free labor. So here I was on a bus to hell.

It was a day before the camp was supposed to start so this was just for the early birds. The kids and CITs that couldn't show up tomorrow. Nine kids and two girl CITs. Tomorrow there would be a hundred and forty campers arriving along with twenty CITs and staff.

Being the typical boy, I checked out the girls immediately. Both about my age, maybe sixteen. The one on the right had long brown hair in a ponytail. Pretty, with discerning eyes. Something told me, rich girl. I don't know. Maybe it was just the attitude.

The one on the left. Shorter, blond, with glasses. Pretty but not as much as ponytail.

I knew what they saw when they looked back at me. A tall guy with a scowl. I had a habit of standing out in a crowd. A fact that always bugged me at my core. I wasn't lanky. More solid. But tall. Six three and I wouldn't see eighteen for another two months.

The rest of the bus had nine kids, eleven to twelve years old, spread out. Five girls and four boys. They were looking at me with shaded frowns. Was I the typical jerk or a special one?

Shifting my backpack on my shoulder, I made my way down the aisle to the end then jerked my thumb for the kid in the back seat to move.

The kid had the good sense to scurry out of the seat.

I plopped down and stared into nothing.

The driver pushed the bus into gear, and we were off. Six weeks I thought. I could do anything for six weeks. It wasn't the end of the world.

Ha, that always makes me laugh. When it comes to being mistaken. No person had ever been more wrong.

The bus crawled through the small town and then started up a switch-back two-lane road into the mountains. I stared out the window at the forest and occasional farm of the Pocono Mountains. Not much different than the area around Syracuse, I thought.

Six weeks I reminded myself. I guess it was better than jail, even if only slightly.

A little over an hour and we finally got there, about twenty-five miles out from the town. I guess this place was farther out than I remembered. When you are a little kid, you don't pick up on things like that. But we were finally there, and things hadn't changed one bit.

About twenty cabins clustered on the far end of the lake. Four main buildings up on a hill above the lake and cabins. On the left, the admin building. Built of thick logs. Next, the combined mess hall and kitchen. Then the showers and restrooms. If I remembered correctly divided down the middle with six showers and eight cubicles on each side. It got busy in the morning, to say the least. And finally, the staff building. More like a dormitory.

Everything was as I remembered it. Even the same float sat in the middle of the lake.

I almost smiled to myself when I remembered the first time, I had swum all the way out there in a race with Billy Jenkins. I wondered where he was. Probably hanging out with his friends, playing video games, or a pick-up basketball game. Things I would end up never knowing. Billy was lost to history. As if he never lived.

I wonder if he'd been playing video games when it all ended. Fighting off monsters while invisible ones ate him up from the inside.

Three sailboats were moored to a pier sticking out into the lake, their sails furled and stowed. The large firepit off to the side looked like it was all ready for hotdogs and smores.

It was the first warm day of summer late spring day. A little cooler up here in the mountains with a high blue sky. But it was the smell though that told me I was somewhere different. A green smell filled with life. Or maybe it was the absence of car exhaust and wet asphalt. Anyway, I took a deep breath and almost relaxed. Then I remembered I was angry at the world and pushed it aside.

The blond and ponytail were waiting for me. The driver Thompson or Thomas or something was rounding up the kids and said he'd be back for us in a minute. The blond stepped forward with a wide smile and I knew the type immediately. She would want to be friends. For life even.

"I'm Brie Osborn," she said holding out her hand.

I shook it, making sure not to apply too much pressure. Mom had gone out of her way to try and make a gentleman out of me. For the most part, she had failed, but some things stuck.

"And this is Jenny," she said indicating the pony-haired girl.

"Jennifer," the girl corrected as she held out her hand.

Again, I made a point of not squeezing too hard. For the briefest moment we stared into each other's eyes, and I saw it immediately. She didn't like me. To her, I was a bug that had dropped onto her plate of food.

I don't know what I'd done. And really, it didn't matter. She wouldn't be the first pretty girl who didn't think I was worth a damn.

Letting go of her hand, I turned away to look out over the camp. Six weeks, I reminded myself and then I was out of here. Two groups of snot-nosed kids to be shepherded.

As I stood there, an awkward silence fell over the three of us. I wanted to smile. They were pretty girls and weren't used to being ignored. But no way was I getting interested. Well, at least not officially.

Thankfully the awkward silence was broken by Thompson returning. He was the manager, I reminded myself. He'd been running this place for years. He had everything down to a system if I remembered correctly. A tight timetable that kept everyone too busy to get into trouble.

I wondered if he knew about me. There had been a police report. But the charges had been dropped when they finally figured out the two other guys were even worse jerks than me. No. He didn't I realized. He would never have accepted Mom's application.

Oh, well. No need to inform him of my past. I'd do my time then go home to finish out my senior year and then off to start some kind of life that I still hadn't figured out.

That memory. Standing there, thinking about the future hurts now. More than you will ever know.

Thompson returned after showing the kids their cabin. He had to be in his late forties with a bit of a paunch. A gray sweatshirt with Camp Tecumseh across the chest and a Yankee's ball cap that looked like it had been dunked in the lake a dozen times.

"Make sure they feel comfortable. Stop the arguments over who gets which bunk. You know stuff like that. Then have them up at the mess hall by five."

Jenny frowned at him. I had determined that I would refer to her as Jenny just to piss her off. "Aren't there any counselors? I thought we were supposed to be learning. You know the whole 'in training' part of things."

The old man had a brief worried look then shook his head. "A couple of them were supposed to show up today. But they got delayed. They'll be here tomorrow along with the rest."

Jenny decided not to push the issue but picked up her backpack and started down the hill. Obviously, she knew where she was going. If I had to guess, I bet she'd been a camper here for ten years and was going through this CIT stuff so she could get on staff next year.

As she walked down the hill, I had to admit her butt was way above average in jeans that were just the right amount of tight.

Thompson caught me checking her out and shook his head before slapping my shoulder. "Don't even think about it."

I laughed for the first time in two weeks. That was going to be an impossibility. I was a seventeen-year-old boy. That was all I thought about.

The blond, Brie, I reminded myself, hurried to catch up with her friend.

Old man Thompson showed me the boy's CIT cabin. On the opposite side of the camp from the girl's CIT cabin. With eighteen cabins for the campers between them. Obviously, these people weren't stupid.

I threw my stuff onto the farthest of eight bunks and wondered what the other CITs would be like. I shrugged my shoulders. I wasn't here to make lifetime friends.

Okay, it couldn't be avoided any longer. I found the cabin with the four boys and entered without knocking. You would have thought that a werewolf had stepped into the place. All four froze, looking at me with wide eyes.

I could see it instantly. Like all boys. At some point in their life they had been bullied by older, bigger boys. The natural instinct was to freeze in the presence of a predator.

Scanning them I saw the usual. Kids. The smallest in the back frowned, but I had to give him credit, he didn't look away.

"I'm Nick," I told them. "I'm supposed to make sure you guys don't get lost on the way to the mess hall. Any problems I need to solve? ... Good. Finish up."

They scrambled to make up their bunks. Sheets and blankets had been left on each one. Once that was done I had them put their stuff away in lockers. They still had that haunted look, waiting for things to go wrong.

"God, lighten up guys," I said. "I won't screw with you. Not unless you deserve it. What are your names?"

"Mike," a chunky kid with red hair said then bit his tongue, obviously wondering if that was the right answer. "Mike Jackson."

Okay. I know I can be intimidating. My size, the fresh scar over my left eyebrow. Oh yeah, and the permanent scowl.

"Carl, Carl Bender," a lanky black kid. Okay, if we had a basketball tournament, I was picking him for my team.

"Anthony, but I prefer Tony. Tony Gallo," A dark-haired Italian kid said as he pushed his glasses back up to the bridge of his nose.

I nodded then turned to the last one. The smallest, and probably youngest. "And you."

The kids finished putting his stuff away, hesitated, then said "Patterson Abercrombie."

The other boys laughed, and I saw the pain shoot behind the kid's eyes. I wondered how many times that had happened in his life and how many times it would in the future. Of course, we all ended up having way worse futures than people laughing at our names. But I didn't know that then so I did what anyone would have done and laughed along with everyone else, but I followed it up by saying, "That's too hard to remember. Besides, a name like that makes you sound like a stockbroker, and you look too intelligent to ever fall into that scam. So I'm going to call you ... Bud. That okay?"

The kid's eyes grew big, and I knew he'd never had a nickname in his entire life. At least not one he liked. Smiling, he nodded.

"Okay," I said as I examined them. "Mike, Carl, Tony, and Bud. God, it sounds like a boy band. You guys break out singing and I'll disown you. I swear."

They laughed and the tension was broken. I wasn't a special jerk, perhaps only a regular one and they could live with that.

Oh, if we had but known what a person could live with and without.

Chapter Two

Jenifer

Camp Tecumseh, God, I loved it. The one place in the world that was safe. Safe from overprotective parents and a judgmental world. No maids reporting to mom every time I broke the slightest rule. I swear I think she paid them extra for every time they ratted me out. Here I could be me. Jennifer O'Brien.

The smells, the colors, the soft breeze. All of it brought back fond memories. And now, finally, I was a CIT. Everything was how it was supposed to be. CIT this summer. Then senior at school next year. After that, either Harvard or Yale. My parents were still arguing about which. But none of that mattered. I was at Camp Tecumseh for the next six weeks and my future was bright.

HA! What a crock of ... stuff that turned out to be.

When we reached the CIT cabin I turned and looked back at that boy going into his cabin. Well, nothing could be perfect. All I could do was shake my head. This Nick person was so wrong for Camp Tecumseh.

I knew the type only too well. A bad boy to his very core. It was obvious, the heavy scowl, the wide shoulders, denim jacket, and the way he talked. As if everyone else in the world was without value. Yes, A definite bad boy.

Unlike most other girls. Bad boys did nothing for me. No fluttering butterflies. No halted breath. No, they were a waste with no socially redeeming value. Especially here.

Deep down, I knew the problem was that he reminded me of my dad. That same cocky attitude and that inability to be faithful. Mom might forgive my dad, but I still couldn't.

Brie glanced to where I was looking and smiled. "It is going to be an interesting summer."

I laughed and shook my head. "Let's hope not. Don't forget. We are here to keep the peace and make sure nothing bad happens."

Well, we failed at that, didn't we? Or at least the world did.

After Brie and I got settled we headed over to the girl's cabin. Brie and I had known each other for eight years. Not bosom buddies. But we'd shared a cabin a couple of times. Been on the same tug-a-war teams that type of thing.

When we got to the girl's cabin we knocked and waited to be let in. Five young girls. Three of them had been here before. The other two were newbies, watching the others to see what to do next.

I was pleased to see bunks being made and things put away in lockers. Eleven and twelve year old's. God, I remembered that awful time of being in between. No longer child, not yet woman. I smiled to myself. It was why girls this age formed such tight bonds with each other. They were the only ones who truly understood.

"I'm Jennifer, this is Brie. We're here if you need any help. Answer any questions."

The five girls stared back, some shrugging before returning to finish their work. I couldn't help but smile. Brie and I were already outsiders. We might be used for information, but we weren't one of them.

An hour on a bus and a shared cabin and they were already forming a team to face the world. After introductions, I watched them for a moment and immediately started putting them into categories.

Ashley Chan, Asian-American. A quick smile and a born helper. She was already assisting Katy Price in finishing with her bunk.

Katy Price, brunet, shy. When I saw her slip a Harry Potter book into her locker I had to smile. Only a true bookworm brings a book to camp. I knew she would have preferred to lay in the shade of a tree and read instead of swimming or games. No, for her, other worlds were her fascination.

Then there was Nicole Parsons. She was easy to figure out. A hint of eyeshadow and lip gloss. Twelve going on sixteen. With a hint of toughness behind her eyes. Nicole was the type of person you didn't want to get on the wrong side of.

Emma Davis, a strawberry blond was watching everyone else with a keen eye. A newbie, she had a natural curiosity. The diary sitting on top of her upper bunk confirmed it. She'd chronicle every detail. Locking onto paper what she couldn't remember.

And finally, Harper Reed. The other first-timer. Confident, not needing to watch the others to know what to do. Tall, pretty on her way to being beautiful. A future heartbreaker. Supermodel in training. A sketchbook slipped under her mattress exposed the secret to her soul. An artist. I wondered if she was any good. Yes, I thought. There was something about Harper that said she would be good at anything she did.

Five young girls. My responsibility. At least until the counselors showed up.

I shook my head. They really should have been here already, getting ready. I was disappointed in them. It was just plain wrong to treat Camp as unimportant. Of course, now it is hard to blame people for being late when they were in the process of dying. It seems sort of petty, if you know what I mean.

After getting everyone settled, we headed up to the mess hall for dinner. The seven of us went through the line for salad, garlic bread, and spaghetti. Not my favorite, but that was the thing about Camp food. You ate what they served, or you went without.

We all sat at a table off to the right. Talking, sharing, an occasional giggle. When the boys showed up, the feeling in the room changed. I couldn't help but shake my head. Even at this young age, the girls were very aware of boys being in the vicinity.

Of course the male members of our species were typical, loud, and rambunctious, with someone throwing a punch at another's shoulder. It was almost as if they were trying to draw attention to themselves. The four of them got their meals and made it a point of sitting as far away as possible.

They wanted attention but didn't want to get contaminated by girls.

Then there was that Nick person. God, what a cold, non-caring, waste of oxygen. He stepped up and Mrs. Smith, the cook, smiled at him as if he were special then gave him a double serving without him having to ask. And of course he skipped the salad entirely.

But it was when he sat down all alone, separate from the boys that I saw his true self. A loner. Most definitely not Camp

Tecumseh material. Oh, well, it was only six weeks.

Again, HA!

The next morning was pretty much the same thing only pancakes instead of spaghetti. It had been a restless night. The newness was already wearing off. The girls had probably stayed up half the night sharing stories about where they were from. Now it was simply a matter of waiting for the other campers to show up so we could get started.

I was trying to organize a volleyball game when Mr. Thompson and Mrs. Smith stepped out of the admin building and called, Brie, myself, and Nick over. The camp manager had a deep frown and kept looking to the front gate. Mrs. Smith simply shook her head.

My stomach clenched up just a bit. I knew that look. It was the look my father got when things didn't go the way he expected. It was just a matter of figuring out who to blame.

"There seems to be a problem," he said with a shake of his head.

The three of us stood there waiting. This could be anything from rat poison in the pancake batter to someone forgetting to order enough toilet paper.

I couldn't help but notice that the Nick person didn't frown. I swear the man could have been told he was to die in an hour, and he wouldn't have cared one way or the other.

"It seems," Mr. Thompson continued. "That some of the staff are still delayed. Mrs. Smith will have to drive the other bus."

It was a little confusing, how did he know they weren't arriving. I knew from long experience that there was no cell coverage up here. Then I suddenly realized that as a result of the changes he meant that there weren't going to be any adults left.

"You guys will have to keep an eye on things."

Okay, I could live with that. A bit better than rat poison.

"Nick, you'll be in charge. Keep them away from the lake and the forest. It will only be a couple of hours."

Mr. Bad boy nodded, as if it was no big deal, being left in charge. I of course wanted to scream, how come he got picked? But I had learned long ago not to challenge older men. It was a waste of time, they never saw reason. My father being a prime example.

"There is stuff to make sandwiches," Mrs. Smith said, "If we're not back in time for lunch. But no using the stove and stay out of the ice cream. That is for special circumstances."

That last line makes me want to both laugh and cry. I'll tell you about it when we get to that part of the story.

Mr. Thompson stared at the front gate for a minute and shook his head Then took a deep breath and nodded for Mrs. Smith to follow him.

We three CITs were joined by the nine campers and stood there to watch the two big yellow buses drive through the front gate.

I think that is the point where my story started. Really. There was my life before and my life after. A life in what used to be the normal world and this life. Believe me, they aren't the same. Not even close.

The End of Everything (The End of Everything 1)

Made in the USA
Coppell, TX
26 November 2024

41069138R00184